The Night Stalkers

Frank's Independence Day

by
M. L. Buchman

Buchman Bookworks

Discover more by this author at: www.buchmanbookworks.com

Cover images:
Red, white and blue fireworks on 4th of July
© Nfsphoto | Dreamstime.com
UH-60 Black Hawk Helicopter-photo ID 120308-A-CD129-001 |
public domain: www.defense.gov
Romantic sunset
© Razihusin | Dreamstime.com
Sparkler © Denys Prokofyev | Dreamstime.com (back cover)

Other works by this author:

M.L. Buchman

The Night Stalkers
The Night Is Mine
I Own the Dawn
Daniel's Christmas
Wait Until Dark
Frank's Independence Day
Peter's Christmas
Take Over at Midnight

...

Angelo's Hearth
Where Dreams are Born
Where Dreams Reside
Maria's Christmas Table

...

Swap Out!

Matthew Lieber Buchman

Nara
The Nara Threshold
The Nara Effect

Second Dark Ages
Monk's Maze

Dieties Anonymous
Cookbook from Hell: Reheated
Saviors 101: the first book of the reluctant Messiah

Dedication

The more I researched this book, the more I came to appreciate the amazing work of the career Foreign Service Diplomats who serve throughout the world. These include Lewis Lukens, the current ambassador to Senegal as of this writing, who does indeed travel frequently to Guinea-Bissau despite its incredible instabilities. This book is dedicated to those brave people striving to make the world a better place.

All African and Central American events occurring prior to this story's setting are as accurate as possible, though this is entirely a work of fiction.

Chapter 1

Frank: July 4, 1988

*F*rank *Adams had his* boys slide up around the metallic-blue late-model BMW at the stop light on Amsterdam Ave. One stood by the passenger door, one ahead, one behind, and he took the driver's window himself as usual.

It was only the third time they'd done this, but Frank saw, without really watching, that they made it look smooth. They'd split the thousand that the chop shop had just paid for the Ford they'd jacked and two grand for the Camry. But a new Beemer? That was a serious score. What they were doing so far uptown this late on a hot, New York night was the driver's own damn fault.

He started it like any standard windshield scam. Spray the windshield to blind the driver, then shake them down for five bucks to clean it so they can see to drive away. The bright bite of ammonia almost reassuring to New Yorkers who had come to expect the scam. He'd long since learned to flick the windshield wiper up so that the driver couldn't just clean their own damn window. It was when the driver's window rolled down, and the person at the wheel started griping, that the real action would begin.

A glance to the sides showed not much traffic. Lot of folks gone down by the water to watch the fireworks, or off with family for July

4th picnics at the park, or on their fire escapes in the sweltering summer heat. The acrid sting of burnt cordite hung like a haze over the city from a million firecrackers, bottle rockets, M-80s, cherry bombs, and everything else legal or not. Hell, Chinatown would be sounding like they were tossing around sticks of dynamite.

Night had settled on the roads out of Columbia University and into his end of Manhattan, and as much darkness as could ever be happening beneath the New York City lights had done gone and happened.

Frank's boys were doing good. At the front and back, they'd leaned casually on the hood and trunk of the car not facing the prize, but instead watching lookout up and down the length of Amsterdam Ave. They'd shout if any cops surfaced.

And no self-respecting BMW driver would run over someone they didn't know just to get away, especially ones who weren't even looking at them threateningly.

Other drivers were accelerating sharply and running the red light just so they weren't a part of whatever was going down at the corner of Amsterdam and midnight.

Three minutes. That meant they had about three minutes until someone nerved down enough to find a pay phone and call the cops and he and his boys had to be gone.

They'd only need about one.

The Beemer jerked back about two feet with little more than a hiss and a throb from that smooth, cool engine.

His boys were on the pavement before Frank could even blink.

Japs had been sitting on the trunk but was now sprawled on his face and Hale sat abruptly on his butt when the car's hood pulled out from underneath him. It was almost funny, the two of them looked so damn surprised.

Then he was facing the rolled down window, just as he'd planned. He could taste the new-car fine-leather smell as it wafted out.

What he hadn't planned was to be staring right down the barrel of a .357. Abruptly, all he could taste was the metal sting of adrenaline and the stink of his own sweat.

He'd seen enough guns to know that the Smith & Wesson 66 was not some normal bad-ass revolver.

He was facing death right between the eyes.

His body froze so hard he didn't even drop the knife nestled out of sight in his palm.

The woman who looked at him, right hand aiming the gun across her body, left hand still on the wheel, had the blackest eyes he'd ever seen. So dark that no light came back from them, like looking down twin barrels of death even more dangerous than the gun's.

A cop siren sounded in the distance, but his boys were already on the move out of there.

"They're leaving you behind."

Her voice was as smooth as her weapon. Calm, not all nervy like someone surprised by a carjacking or unfamiliar with the weapon she held rock steady.

"What I told 'em to do."

"Don't risk the whole team?"

He shrugged a yes.

That siren was getting louder and it was starting to worry him. But even doing a drop and run, well… He was fast, but not faster than a .357. He stayed put. Classy lady in a Beemer and a dead carjacker, she wasn't risking any real trouble if she gunned him down where he stood.

"Decision point. Go down for it. Spend some time in juvie—"

"I'm twenty, twenty-one next week." Why'd he been dumb enough to say that? Not that the cops wouldn't find out, but they didn't have his prints anywhere in their system… yet. He didn't carry any ID either, but there was only so long you could play that card.

"Okay, do some time or get in the car."

He looked into the deep well of those dark eyes, allowing himself three heartbeats to decide what the hell she was up to. The sharp squeal of cop tires swerving around some other car too few blocks away won the argument.

Frank moved around the front of the car fast, flicking down the wiper blade as he went, and slid into her passenger seat.

While he circled, she'd shifted the big gun into her left hand. Could shoot with either hand, that took training. Some off duty cop in a Beemer, just his luck.

He was barely in the car when the fuzz rounded the corner, their lights going.

"Buckle up."

It was only after he buckled in that another thought struck him. A bad one. She just might drive him somewhere, gun him down, and dump his body. Never knew with cops in this town. Then she wouldn't even have to fill out any damn paperwork. *Little bit late to think of that shit,*

Adams. Dumbass! Once around the passenger side, he should have just kept running, not climbed into the lady's damn car like a whatever it was that went to the slaughter. Sheep? Calves? Something. Frank Adamses.

She slid the gun under the flap of her leather vest so that it was out of sight, but still aimed at him across her body. She ran the windshield wiper and together they watched the blue-and-white roll up fast. The cops pulled up driver to driver, facing the wrong way on the street to do so.

"Everything okay, ma'am?"

Frank had the distinct impression that even though the woman was reassuring the cop, if Frank so much as flinched, there'd be a big, bad hole in his chest and that the thing that would really tick her off was the damage to her German-engineered car door where the bullet would punch a good-sized hole after making a real mess of his body on its way through. It took her long enough to talk the cop down that Frank had time to register how the car's seat fit to his body. It was way more comfortable than any chair or sofa he'd ever slouched in. Damn seat alone probably cost more than everything he owned.

Finally satisfied, only after blinding Frank with a big flashlight a couple of times, the cops rolled away real slow. He'd purposely dressed okay in his best jeans and a loose button-down shirt he'd worn to Levon's courtroom wedding. That way he wasn't too scary for the windshield-washing scam to work. It paid off now, he didn't look too out of place in this classy car. He eyed the woman carefully, as classy looking as her vehicle. Or even more.

She pulled her hand out from under her vest of dark leather even finer than the seat upholstery, leaving the gun behind, and rolled up the window. Shoulder holster. He'd tried to carjack a woman who wore a .357 in a shoulder holster. What were the chances of that kind of bad luck? Well, one in three. Third carjacking ever, woman with large gun. Not exactly high-level math.

Though he'd never heard of anything like it on the street. He'd been told to watch for crazies, diving for glove compartments and purses, so full of nerves that they were more danger to themselves than anyone else. Best advice on those had been to run. Toward the back of the car. Make yourself a hard shot when they're all buckled in and facing forward. They'd be undertrained, have lousy aim, and probably wouldn't shoot if they thought they'd won. That's if they could find the damn safety.

Not this lady. Cool and calm.

He'd bet she could execute his ass without havin' a bad night's sleep.

"Let's go somewhere and talk." With the window up, the air-con dropped the temperature about twenty degrees from the July heat blast going on out in the real world which was sweet, but left a chill up his spine that started right where his butt was planted in the fine leather seat.

She punched the gas and popped the clutch, in seconds they were hurtling downtown on Amsterdam and Frank knew he better hang on for dear life.

Chapter 2

Frank: July 2nd, Now

That's how I met Beat, Agent Beatrice Ann Belfour of the United States Secret Service." Frank Adams hung tight onto the fold-down arms of his seat aboard the Marine One chopper. He'd recently learned to despise helicopters.

President of the United States Peter Matthews burst out laughing and Frank, now the head of his Presidential Protection Detail, did his best not to feel foolish. It wasn't even his usual, engaging, buddy-buddy laugh. The man thought he was being downright hilarious.

"You got into the Secret Service by trying to carjack a Secret Service Agent?" He managed to gasp it out between guffaws like the American public never got to hear on TV.

"It's not like she had a sign on her damn Beemer saying, 'Federal Agent, Don't Screw with Me'." Frank had to speak up to be heard over the pounding rotors of the chopper and the President's laughter.

He'd learned that while this President didn't swear, he liked the chummy feeling of occasional curse words from others, as long as it didn't go too far.

The last President had been the opposite, cursing a blue streak in private but expecting no one else to say so much as "darn." And then only if they'd been very recently shot.

The Presidential White Hawk had better sound insulation than your standard Sikorsky Black Hawk, but it still wasn't quiet. It also had about two tons more armor than any other chopper flying, which Frank appreciated since it was his job to keep the man riding in it alive. But he'd rather be in anything than a chopper, especially a Black Hawk. Frank had barfed his guts out on a simulated-combat flight with the Special Operations Aviation Regiment, the 160th of the U.S. Army's Special Forces, and hoped he'd never have to fly with the Night Stalkers again. He'd take the Marines in the White Hawk any day.

Out of well-trained habit, he scanned the blue skies outside the chopper. The New Jersey shoreline lay below, and not much else except the morning sunshine sparkling off the rolling Atlantic. The window was hazy due to the thickness of the bulletproof glass. It would stop anything up to fifty caliber and it would do its best to stop that, too.

They were in transit from D.C. for a meeting at the United Nations. This flight was also way more secure than that training mission had been six months ago. Not only had they been simulating combat, who knew choppers could roll over and dive upside down, but they'd been far away from the usual bubble that surrounded the Commander-in-Chief. Sure, they'd been traveling with two of the most heavily-armed helicopters on the planet and with Henderson and Beale, the two best pilots the U.S. Army Special Forces had ever created, but still… No one except those on the flight had even technically known the President was aboard and they'd crossed half the country with only Frank beside him.

For this trip, Frank felt much more comfortable. They were Number Two of two in a flight of identical VH-60N White Hawks. The other bird was there to confuse any potential attacker as to which craft the President actually flew in. The pilots had switched the lead several times to deceive anyone trying to track them. A trio of well-armed Cobras flew escort on the White Hawks.

On top of that, air traffic controllers were keeping the skies clear of any other flights for a box that extended five miles behind them and to either side, and ten miles ahead. Any aircraft that entered that box would rapidly receive attention from the Cobras. In seconds more, intruders would also be facing the pair of F/A-18 Super Hornet fighter jets and the F/A-18 Growler, an electronic-warfare version of the Hornet, all flying out of Langley Air Force Base and presently lurking another twenty-thousand feet above the choppers.

Unlike that training mission, this flight was also unlikely to include any aerobatics maneuvers. Yet another thing to be deeply grateful for the Marines flying this machine.

He was seated backwards in the White Hawk, sitting opposite the forward-facing President. No one else was in the aircraft's cabin other than the two pilots seated in the cockpit over Frank's shoulder. Frank glanced behind him, but they both appeared alert and focused forward. President Matthews sat at ease in the narrow, brown leather armchair just like Frank's own. His hair, the longest of any occupant of the Oval Office in a couple hundred years, clearly marked the youngest President in history. His dark hair flowed to his collar and his deep brown eyes radiated both intelligence and humor. The television cameras just loved this man.

Frank's wide shoulders didn't fit the narrower helicopter seats nearly as well as the President's. And at six-foot-two, the low ceiling of the White Hawk's cabin was disconcertingly close. He kept his seatbelt cinched tightly for the entire hour flight so that he wouldn't bang his head if they hit an air pocket.

"So, how did you enjoy being taken, uh, into custody?"

"Well," Frank scanned out the window again. "I managed to not crap my pants on her nice leather, but it was a close thing. You remember how Tommy Lee recruited Will Smith in *Men in Black?* The secret world, the bench, the change-your-whole-life lecture, and all that?"

The President nodded.

"It was just like that. When that movie hit after I'd been in the Service for about a decade, it was like a bad drug flashback without ever having done any drugs to earn it."

Chapter 3

Beatrice: 1988

United States Secret Service Agent Beatrice Ann Belfour looked over at the kid sitting in her BMW's passenger seat. She was only three years older than he was, but she couldn't help thinking of him as a kid. A young street punk. But not just a young street punk. If he had been, he'd be locked in the back of the blue-and-white cruiser of the NYPD at this very moment.

Beatrice had only been an agent of the Secret Service for a year. And only authorized to enter the field and carry a weapon since last week. Good timing. She rubbed her palm against the steering wheel, thankful for the absorbent leopard-spotted steering wheel cover that her little niece had insisted she purchase. Beatrice's hands were not steady, but she certainly couldn't show that to this kid.

She should have just turned him over, but there'd been indicators that intrigued her. And a significant portion of her training had been learning to trust her instincts. Her problem, she was often told, was that her instincts were also crazy stupid, but that wasn't any news to her.

He hadn't flinched when she'd pulled her weapon, hadn't even dropped the knife he thought was so carefully tucked out of sight. That showed a steadiness of nerves. He'd worked up a carjacking scam with the guys sitting on the hood and trunk acting as both spotters and deterrents.

That was a scenario that she hadn't been briefed on in training. Similar yes, but not the same. It was a good twist. He'd even trained them to run at trouble to minimize losses, which made him a team player as well as a good leader. Clearly all of this was his idea. Even the attention to detail as he dropped the wiper blade back into place, despite the distraction of the muzzle of her S&W 66 staring him between the eyes, spoke to his ability to remain focused under stress.

Even most junior agents didn't do as well in practice scenarios and for this guy, it had been live.

"If you can make your hands work," she'd bet they were shaking like Gene Wilder in *Blazing Saddles* when he was needing a drink. "You can put that knife and any other hardware you're carrying into the glove compartment. They won't like you carrying where we're going."

"Only have the knife." His voice was deep and resonant as befit someone with a chest his size. She guessed six-two, two-ten or two-hundred-and-twenty pounds, and none of it fat.

No gun. Maybe he couldn't afford it, which seemed unlikely in the neighborhood she'd found him in. You'd think a woman would be safe driving down a New York street six lanes wide, bright under the lights. He probably didn't carry because he knew penalties went way up if something went wrong and he was picked up packing a firearm.

He held the knife up for her to see, his hand didn't shake much at all, less than hers would be if she took them off the wheel. Not a switchblade, nor a spring-load, but it had a heavy blade she'd bet he could flick open one-handed. Again, legal. Not by a lot, but it would pass for a standard pocket knife under the New York criminal code. She'd bet no one else on his crew was carrying even that. He ran his team as clean and legally deniable as possible.

He popped the glove box with the back of his thumb and wiped the knife on his pants before dropping it in and knocking the little door closed with his knee. No gloves, which would have stood out on the mid-summer night, so he was limiting where he left fingerprints. She made a bet with herself that he'd use a shirttail to wipe the seatbelt buckle and the door handle as he exited the car.

This kid was careful. Which reaffirmed her first instincts.

At this time of night she made it all the way downtown in under twenty minutes and the guy didn't say a word. Halfway there, she'd asked his name.

"Frank."

No last name offered. He didn't look nervy, again just being careful.

She flew down to 7 World Trade Center and whipped into the downward-spiraling ramp of the underground parking garage with a bright squeal of tires. Her parents had given her the car as a make-up present when she'd been named a field agent last week. She'd retired the very old gray Honda, probably only days before its final collapse. She'd named it Witherspoon, for what she thought Michael Caine might have called his Aston Martin in *The Italian Job*. She was thinking of naming her new BMW Jean Claude, after Van Damme's kicking performance in *Bloodsport*. But that had only been released a few months ago and didn't have the classic feel of the 1969 heist movie. She'd find its name eventually.

Her parents felt that a federal job was beneath their only daughter. They'd worked hard to get out of the same poor-ass neighborhood where she'd just found Frank. That their daughter hadn't taken her Columbia University education to become a doctor or lawyer, or at least marry one, had made them more than a little bit crazy. After a year of simultaneously completing her Secret Service training and managing to finish her degree in criminal law, they'd felt contrite and given her the Beemer. She wasn't any less pissed at them for all the hassle they'd dished out over the last year, but she did love this car.

It practically stood on its nose when she hammered the brakes at the control booth of the restricted section of the underground parking. She lowered the window.

"Hi Beatrice," Harry popped the button inside his booth to raise the steel gate and lower the tire punchers into the pavement surface. "Knew it was you when I heard the wheels hit the upper ramp."

She flashed her ID at him for form's sake. Added a grin of thanks and goosed the gas, spinning down two more layers to her assigned spot.

Beatrice kept an eye out as the kid climbed out of the car. Sure enough, Frank applied his shirttail to belt buckle and both the inside and outside door handles.

# # #

"Any record?"

Frank didn't "huh" this lady as he tucked his shirt back in as smoothly as he could. Didn't pretend to not understand. He looked at her over the top of her car, kinda surprised at how far down he had to look. She'd seemed so damn big with the fancy car, the shiny damn gun, and the total lack of fear. She couldn't stand more than five-seven or eight, but there was no question which of them was holding the power at the moment.

And he didn't like that it was her. Not one lousy little bit.

He shook his head. No record, no time, no juvie.

"Not even detention, much."

He'd been top twenty at the high school, which only said he wasn't as out-and-out lazy as everyone else there. College hadn't been all that high on anyone's to-do list in his class. He'd had some idea that the chop shops might eventually pay him enough to hit Columbia or City University, but he'd never figured that as real likely.

The "no detention" line got a laugh he hadn't expected, and he had to reassess her again. Bright white teeth, and hair as dark and shining as those eyes. The smile also made her look younger than the thirty he'd originally tagged her with. Low twenties. He moseyed around the rear of the car and tried to make no big deal out of checking her up and down.

Red Converse sneakers and faded jeans that showed hard use and good quality. Certainly not Goodwill or Woolworths. High-necked yellow blouse. Black leather vest, dressy kind that wasn't for warmth, but instead for looks… and hiding damn big guns. The combo promised a slender waist and a serious enough chest that the gun in the shoulder holster didn't show much under the soft leather. If he didn't know it was there, he might not have thought anything out of place. And a whole lot of things were in the right place on this woman.

"Do I pass?"

He went for a safe shrug. Okay, so he hadn't pulled off much in the way of smooth, but she was a woman who deserved a long look.

"Turn around." She didn't make it a request.

He narrowed his eyes at her and she twirled a finger. Well, he knew that his looks didn't leave him nothing to worry about in that department. He and his boys worked out together every day 'cause there sure wasn't shit else to do in the projects, and he'd received more than his fair share of fine benefits from the ladies to keep him working the iron.

"Describe what I'm wearing."

Some kinda test. So, he stared at the row of cars parked across the way, lined up neat as bowling pins. They were all driven by skilled drivers like her, each car slid into its spot sweet and straight. This wasn't no office-bozo kinda parking. The garage was all pretty quiet on this side of that security gate up there. Not much in the way of traffic. 'Course it was one in the morning on July Fourth. The place smelled of garage, oil, fuel, and rubber. Where the hell was he?

So, he described her. Got into it. She'd left a damn clear impression. She didn't stop him after her clothing, so he got into her high cheekbones and full lips, her black hair, long, straight but threatening to curl madly, and the thin gold chain around her neck with no ornament dangling on it. And she didn't need anything more to look seriously fine. No rings or bracelets and...

He spotted a reflected motion on the flat rear glass of a Ford Bronco parked across the way.

Her reflection pulling out that damn big gun.

He dove for the ground and rolled between a couple of cars.

Sweat poured off him even as he regained his feet in a low squat and began thinking on the best direction to run. Blown away in a parking gara—

That laugh again. It stopped him cold.

She wandered around the car until she was facing him, hands empty. Out where he could see them plainly. Did nothin' to calm his nerves.

"You recall what you see accurately, are exceptionally aware of your surroundings, and have good reaction time."

"Which means what?" He managed to make it come out more as an angry shout he meant than the choked squeak he was feeling. He stood slowly, his heart still pounding against his ears.

"Which means I was right. Let's go."

She walked off toward the steel-faced garage elevator set in an unadorned concrete wall. He glared at the low pipes wandering along the garage ceiling, but finding no kinda clue up there, he followed her.

#

Beatrice pressed the button that brought the elevator down, but didn't say a word. She stayed quiet to let Frank stew in his own juices. He stalked into the elevator like a grizzly bear who'd just crawled out of its den and found no food anywhere. Seriously grumpy. She keyed in the lock code to take them up to the seventh floor.

"You like being right." Frank didn't make it a question and he didn't waste time asking her where they were going.

Beatrice had to grant that the kid had the patience to figure out that he'd find that out soon enough. And also enough smarts to know that she wasn't likely to tell him before then.

"Damn straight!" She loved the feeling. "Being right is fun. It's one of my favorite things. And if I were blond and could sing, I'd be Julie Andrews."

His look told her that his education in movies needed some serious fixing up.

For the life of her she couldn't figure out why she so enjoyed messing with this kid.

Kid. He was seven inches taller than she was with a workout chest big enough that he made the elevator feel small. Nor had she missed how fine a form he had when he'd turned away from her. That she'd even noticed was interesting in itself, but she absolutely wasn't going to think about that.

The door opened and they stepped into the inner building's lower entrance foyer, the one which lay seven stories above the front-entrance street-level signs for brokerages and banks that filled the bulk of 7 World Trade Center, New York, New York.

Frank grunted when he saw the sign above the desk. But no more than that. Steel letters on dark wood: United States Secret Service. She remembered the feeling the first time she'd seen this sign, as if the world had just become a great deal more serious. Of course that had been on her new recruit tour, she'd known what building she was in. She gauged Frank's reaction. "Adapts rapidly to changing situations," was added to her initial assessment.

He eyed her sideways for a moment, then nodded to himself as if she finally made sense in his world. Of course a Secret Service agent would outsmart a simple carjacking scheme.

She'd spent the last year training in driving, weapons, investigations, research, and a dozen other skills. She'd also been trained in unarmed combat and wanted to see how Frank Adams did. It was stupid to take on an unknown street fighter twice her size, which made it just her style.

She signed in at the desk and signaled one of the guys to come out and pat Frank down, which he submitted to but clearly didn't like.

"Escort him through. Find him some sweats." She glanced down. His feet were as big as the rest of him and there probably weren't any loaners that size. "Barefoot is fine."

She turned and headed into the women's locker room to change. She considered handing him to someone else for testing, which is exactly why she didn't. Her instructors were always telling her she was much too impulsive, too quick to leap into the fray. But one of the old-timers, one who actually used to ride on President Ford's protection detail, the only PPD agent she'd met so far, told her never to stop doing that. From then on she ignored all instructions to back off and had graduated top of her class. Maybe it was part of some test to see if she'd comply. She hadn't.

She wandered into the gym. They told her it was nothing as nice as the one in D.C., but it worked fine for her. A row of weight machines down one side and a gray foam mat that covered the rest of the floor. She knew from experience that it wasn't as soft as it looked.

When Frank arrived, he looked amazing. The black t-shirt with large white U.S.S.S. stretched tight across his chest and showed actual six-pack abs. Black gym shorts revealed legs that rippled with muscle. She could feel the heat rising through her body, so she turned away and led him onto an open corner of the mat.

He tried to turn so that it was his back facing the wall, rather than hers, but she didn't let him. It left him watching the other agents over his shoulder, keeping an eye on them. There were only a couple working out. Things were quiet on July Fourth night, these few were probably just killing time before their shift started. She knew one of them well enough to wave, but that was all.

She herself was glad of the reason to be missing the party at her parents. That was the main reason she'd been cruising up to Columbia to check on a posted summer class schedule she could have just as easily called on tomorrow.

"Hit me."

Frank goggled at her so she repeated herself.

"Ladies first," he replied.

She shot a rabbit punch at his sternum without hesitating. She'd thought to drop him as a lesson, but her fist mostly bounced off a tight gut, though the breath did whoosh out of him. He'd also managed to twist enough to make it a partially glancing blow.

Beatrice went for another punch and Frank, predictably, went for the block.

But she didn't land the punch, instead she went low and swept his leg.

On his way down, he was fast enough to snag a hand behind her leg and take her down as well. She landed on top of him and almost got the nerve pinch on his hand, but he was strong enough to wrench free, despite the pain that must have caused.

They pushed off each other and rolled to their feet.

"Damn," Frank shifted lightly on his feet circling.

Now he was going to be predictable and gripe about surprise attacks. "You smell wonderful."

It flustered her enough that when he went for the takedown, she landed hard on her back before she could recover.

Frank knocked the air right out of her.

Chapter 4

Frank: Now

I can't begin to tell you how good that lady was," Frank massaged his chin where Beatrice's elbow had surprised him twenty-five years before, after he'd slammed her to the mat. Even now, he could remember the scent of her as clearly today as if no time had passed at all. Like midnight and roses. Dark, mysterious, and lush.

And then she'd clipped his chin with her elbow and planted his face in that stone-hard mat of the Secret Service gym.

The White Hawk was circling down to the Manhattan Downtown Heliport. Nine a.m., exactly on schedule. Frank looked down to check the dock.

They'd cleared the pier of other flights. A quick scan below showed that the police boats had cordoned off the part of the East River that flowed by the heliport.

The heliport itself was a pier and a barge near the south tip of Manhattan. The tiny parking lot off South Street that could hold about a dozen cars was presently blocked by half-a-dozen black Secret Service SUVs. They'd closed a short section of the street, and the rest of the Presidential motorcade waited for them including a pair of Humvees with turret guns and an ambulance, surrounded by a phalanx of New York's finest mostly on motorcycles.

A long pier stuck out from the shore separated from the land by the terminal building. His earpiece confirmed what his eyes could see. The "all secure" mirrored by the agents in dark gray suits standing watch outside the terminal's doors. The long pier stretched out into the East River. Brooklyn rose on the far shore, bridges soaring above the boat traffic on the bright water. The four helipads were empty, and a pair of Beasts, the Presidential limousines, were parked there. Then the big barge, that looked little different from the pier, floated to the north. About a third of the ten helicopter parking spots on the barge were taken, but the only guys near them were agents.

"Merlin inbound," Frank announced over the radio.

President Matthews grinned at him as he did every time he heard his Secret Service codename. If the main man got a kick out of being dubbed a wizard, that was fine with Frank. And it fit. Youngest President in history, he'd fostered more peace accords than anyone had pulled off in a whole lot of terms. Halfway through his first term and he'd already visited the United Nations more times than any other prior President in their entire incumbency.

And being there on July second, right before the July Fourth holiday would look good in the press. He knew that wasn't what motivated the Man, but neither was he going to be stupid and miss the chance to leverage the opportunity a bit.

They circled as they descended toward the pier, providing Frank one last look in all directions. Nothing caught his eye, nothing pulled his attention. The only thing he noticed was that the ambulance was behind the rearmost Humvee. It was supposed to be in front so that the Humvee's gunner would have a clear field of fire and the ambulance would be inside the bubble with the President if they had to crash down a defensive perimeter. He called down and they started shuffling it as the Marine One chopper settled at the outmost spot on the main pier, the most defensible spot.

"Check the drivers, ambulance and Humvee. They should both know better."

As the wheels kissed the pier, the answer came back into his earpiece. "Ambulance broke down, they had to send their second team. Rolled in late, but they're on my cleared list." Then after a brief pause. "He won't forget next time." He could hear the laugh in Hank Henson's voice. Hank took deep pleasure in making rookies suffer. Probably been hell on new pledges at whatever Ivy League fraternity he'd belonged to. Frank had done night school at NYU.

Even before the chopper's rotors stopped, Beast Two was backing up close to the door. They alternated which was the decoy car. Once the rotors halted, a Marine opened the side door which rolled toward the back. Frank stepped out first, scanned once more, receiving nods from the key agents.

Second day of July in New York City. The heat rolled across him like an old friend, hot, thick with flavor, the smell of home. No other city smelled like it. He tugged at the jacket of his custom-tailored suit to make sure it both hid his weapon and offered easy access. Damn suits cost a fortune, but he didn't look armed in them, so it was worth it. No need to remind the President more than necessary that he was surrounded by armed men every minute of the day.

He let Merlin down, making sure he was between the President and the bulk of the Manhattan buildings. Two more agents to either side flanked him for the thirty-foot walk to the car. Human shield in place.

In moments, he and Merlin were locked in and the motorcade was moving. That was one of the secrets of Presidential security, never stay still, a moving target was much harder to hit.

Frank hated this next stretch. For the next four-point-one miles there was no question about where the Presidential motorcade would be. There were alternate routes through the city. However, up the FDR was the safest and fastest, but it meant being predictable.

"You said meeting Beatrice Belfour was like *Men in Black?"* President Peter Matthews was ignoring whatever crises he carried in his briefcase. He'd snapped it shut halfway through the flight and asked Frank about how he'd ended up head of the PPD. Boss' prerogative.

Main Man wanted to talk? Then Frank would. Wanted to play Scrabble? He'd play Scrabble, and lose horribly no matter how hard he tried. It was the President's secret vice, he loved strategy, he played online in competitions and often finished in the money at tournaments. He was always harassing Frank about finding some way for him to compete in the National Scrabble Championship, but you had to show up in person for that.

Frank had almost crapped his pants laughing when Beale had told him the origin of his preferred anonymous player identity, Sneaker Boy. Had to do with Beale chucking the President, back when he was much younger, into the Reflecting Pool in D.C. while wearing brand new sneakers. He'd have paid good money to see that.

And now the President wanted to talk.

Frank let his guard down, as much as he ever did when riding with the Man. Locked inside the Beast with the President, security was someone else's issue. Mostly. There was only so long that you could stay on alert, so he relaxed as much as he could when he wasn't front and center.

"Well, yeah. She showed me this whole weird world behind the magic curtain, training gym, high-rise offices, high-tech communication war rooms that could span the globe. Then we sat right over there." He pointed out the right-hand window across to where a small park wrapped around the Brooklyn side of the Brooklyn Bridge.

He took a cold bottle of water from the small cooler and knocked it back. July first and it was high-nineties in the city. What was August going to be like? At least it hadn't stunk of garbage. When he'd met Beat it had been so damn hot that the city didn't need a garbage strike in order to reek of it.

Chapter 5

Frank: 1988

They filmed Moonstruck *here* last year." Beatrice told him as they sat side by side on the park bench and looked out at the East River and Manhattan shimmering in the nighttime heat steaming off the water's surface. Once again in their street clothes, he couldn't help remembering her in her workout gear. Her chest gave the big, white U.S.S.S. logo a whole new meaning. No vest hiding curves that really needed to be seen and appreciated. And legs, damn but the woman had amazingly serious legs.

"Moonstruck." Frank had no idea what she was talking about. He just knew his chin still hurt like hell, it was two a.m., and he was sweating like a pig because the temperature hadn't broken in almost two weeks. And he knew that Beatrice was limping bad on the right and trying not to show it. Damn but she was tough. No whining at all though they were both sore. "What's that?"

"Boy, we've got to do something about your movie education. It is seriously lacking."

Movie? He looked around the dock. It didn't look like much. It stuck out a little ways into the East River, Manhattan and the Brooklyn Bridge made for an amazing skyline, from the Twin Towers right up to Roosevelt Island. Here there was just water, warped old wood on the

27

dock, and a couple of steel benches so clean that tourists must come here. Sure weren't no benches this clean in his neighborhood. To the south was a small park. To the north, a fancy restaurant all closed and dark inside, though the perimeter lights were on so it would be hard to sneak around. He spotted a couple of security cameras up high, but they didn't have cables to them. Fakes. Dumb fakes. He knew some boys into smash-and-grab, maybe he should tip them off.

"So what movies did you see?"

What was it with this woman and movies? *"Platoon* kicked ass."

"Okay, it did. I'll give you that one."

"Uh, Stallone was good."

"Rambo III. Like two weren't enough. Sequels are a waste of celluloid. We really gotta do something about this. You're a walking disaster."

"What? First, you're dissing my man Sly. And now you're gonna make another weak-ass attempt to kick my ass or something?"

That got a smile out of her. He seriously liked that smile. And he'd bet if he tried to do anything about trying to kiss it, he'd end up with a faceful of dock splinters.

"That will be up to you."

Whether or not he got to kiss her? No. He shook his head. Whether or not she tried to kick his ass.

Beatrice looked out over the water. Tide was coming in so it smelled of salt and the Atlantic rather than old diesel fuel and other crap that floated down the river when the tide was running.

"I think you've got what it takes. The United States Secret Service is not for the weak of heart. We've got two mandates. Money laundering, counterfeiting, and fraud is the first. Then there's head-of-state protection. All dangerous as can be. That's if they let you in. First they'll do so much investigating on you that an alien crawling out of your chest would be a relief. They'll know so much about you that you won't know what hit you."

While he had a weak spot for Sigourney in too little clothes packing a serious damn gun, the thought of what an investigation would dig up about him sent a chill up his back. He'd just twice committed grand theft auto by carjacking. That wouldn't go down good at all if they found out.

"I, uh, don't think that's gonna be happening."

"I know I wasn't your first carjack. You were too sure of yourself."

"Until you stuck that damn gun in my face."

"Until I stuck my gun in your face. But what you've got going for you is rarer than you think. It's also a way out of your present mess. I've been an agent for a year and it's awesome. I learned enough to stop you."

Frank considered that while a tugboat worked its way against the tide, a long barge of gravel piled in tall mounds trailing far behind. She had stopped him, stopped him cold. If there was ever a good advertisement for what she was sellin', she was it. The woman looked and smelled amazing, and had almost beat his ass on the wrestling mat. He sure wasn't going to think about how good she'd felt in his arms even as she'd planted a knee in his gut and he'd had to partly sprain her ankle to get her off him.

"So why did you join?"

"I'm going to be on the Presidential Protection Detail some day."

"Why there?" He tried to picture that. Riding with the Main Man. Sure, and catching a bullet so that he didn't. Frank had seen enough gunshot wounds and deaths to last him a hundred times his twenty years. Wouldn't find him steppin' in front of no bullets on purpose.

"Because the PPD are the very best on the planet."

"And you're just that damn good."

"Damn straight."

He gave her a knowing smirk. But the thing was, he believed her.

Chapter 6

Frank: Now

Then she left it up to me whether or not I showed up the next day to start filling out the paperwork."

The President smiled. "But you're the one heading up my Protection Detail."

"Yeah," Frank returned the smile. He'd gotten the assignment when Peter Matthews announced he was running. They didn't start guarding the candidates that soon, but they started studying and planning and he'd pulled the duty detail on that. By the time the D.C. native became a Presidential contender, Frank was on him. When he was elected, President-elect Matthews had asked to have him stay on.

"Yeah, heading your detail... Kinda pisses her off." He grinned. When they were alone, he knew the casual helped the President relax, as if he were with a friend rather than his bodyguard. But now they were rolling up the semi-circular drive in front of the main building of the U.N. He threw the mental switch... back into agent mode.

A voice in his ear reminded him, "Entering Turtle Bay." Turtle Bay, which probably hadn't seen a turtle since it was named back in the 17th century, was the Manhattan neighborhood that included the United Nations Headquarters and often referred to just the U.N. section of it.

"You're a brave man, Frank Adams." The President didn't even glance out at the phalanx of agents ensuring the front entrance was secure for their arrival. "I don't think that Agent Beatrice Ann Belfour is someone I'd want to 'piss off' even a little bit."

"Well, I'll admit, she has her more dangerous moments. The woman knows no fear."

"Nor do you," the President checked his tie and jacket. Today it was a sharp gray with a garish red-and-white Washington Nationals tie. He was known for his ties and his love of the D.C. baseball team. Frank had accompanied him to more than one game and watched him eat ballpark hotdogs until any normal man would be sick. It always struck him as funny that the Harvard and Oxford graduate, leader of the country, always so calm and collected, could scream and rant about bad calls against his home team.

"You wear that tie around New York, Mr. President, there's nothing I can do to protect you from a Yankees fan. Just so you know."

"Good thing we aren't technically in New York then."

The U.N. grounds were extraterritorial, subject only to the laws of the U.N., rather than the U.S. and the city of New York. They'd just left the country right, in the middle of Manhattan, which had always cracked him up.

Frank nodded for him when the President had the gray suit straightened-around just right, like a human mirror.

"I've never seen you show a moment of fear," the President grabbed his briefcase and glanced around to make sure he'd left no papers behind.

"Well, sir, you didn't see the color of my pants after we climbed off Major Emily Beale's Black Hawk helicopter on that flight. Fear may only be a seven-point word, but I sure felt it that day."

A last laugh for the President before he entered the fray of international politics.

A voice in his ear called the, "All clear." Frank could see the agent outside ready to open the Beast's door, over a hundred pounds of armor and bullet-proof glass.

"You ready, sir?"

"Ready for an entire day and evening of arguing with China and Russia over the latest North Korean fiasco, and trying to calm down Myanmar about the Thai raids into their poppy fields, and… Sure. Can't wait."

"Do it." Frank announced into the wrist microphone of his radio.

The agent standing beside the car swung open the door.

Chapter 7

Frank: 1988

The car door caught Frank sharply on the knees and he tumbled back. It was a ratty 1967 Ford Fairlane, peeling white paint, Alabama plate number four-three-seven-five-something, hard to see in the moonlit semi-darkness.

It hadn't looked like any trouble. Just a driver. Another Secret Service trainee, Jake Hellman, had him covered.

Frank had gone to the back door of the beater car and someone lying on the floor had kicked the door open, hard, just as he'd looked in. He'd fallen on his ass just like Hale at the carjacking. He fell on the red Georgia dirt of the Federal Law Enforcement Training Center.

Then his shins stung like hell as the lower edge of the door scraped across them.

He shot out a palm strike and rammed it full force against the car door before its edge could scrape off his kneecaps. That at least stopped the excruciating progress of the swinging steel along his shins. With his other hand he managed to shove off the ground, into a roll, and slam his shoulder against the door, snapping it shut.

Whoever was playing the perpetrator in the car hadn't expected that. A woman's squeak sounded through the front window that the driver had rolled down when Frank and Jake stopped the Fairlane for inspection.

Agent Beatrice Ann Belfour. Had to be.

Hadn't seen her in weeks, different agents rotated through the FLETC training scenarios. But she was always causing him pain when she was down here.

He yanked out his gun and rolled up to kneel on the hard-packed, deeply rutted earth. That was a big, damn mistake, his shins screamed.

No live ammo in the gun, he couldn't shoot out the window.

Instead, he rapped the glass sharply with the butt of his gun, right where he'd glued on a bit of shattered spark-plug ceramic.

The safety glass practically dissolved, now instead of hard glass, the ceramic had triggered the safety glass into shattering. It was now a loose, wavering sheet, opaque with tiny crack lines and barely holding together. Old car-thief trick.

He shifted to his feet, swallowing the hiss of pain, and slapped the friable glass with his elbow.

The window disappeared in a shower of tiny pieces.

Even as he aimed his weapon into the car, Beatrice kicked the door again.

This time he had his hip against it and all her violent kick did was force her to slide the other way and smack her head on the far door. He couldn't see her clearly in the shadows, but there was no question in his mind.

"You, Agent Belfour, are under arrest for bloodying an agent of the United States Secret Service." He could feel the hot blood trickling down his shins. The long scrapes were already stinging with the sharp salt he'd been sweating from every pore since the moment he'd landed in Georgia three months before.

In answer she popped open the far door she'd just banged her head on and tumbled out the other side of the car and into the dark.

He dove over the trunk and managed to snag her by the ankle before she could sprint into the night. She was clearly the target of interest, the driver probably just a driver. And not his concern at the moment. There were big-picture moments, and stay-focused moments. Stopping Beatrice was definitely in the second category.

Already moving forward fast, his grip around her ankle and her forward momentum slammed her to the ground.

"Ow! Crap! That hurt."

"Welcome to my world, Beat—" That's when she flipped around to get him in a headlock between her knees.

It took three tries, but he managed to find the pressure point on her thigh that had her writhing away before she'd quite choked all the air out of him.

He managed to stand and lean forward to grab her just as she shot to her feet to run again.

The top of her head and his nose intersected.

It was mostly luck that he snagged an arm around her waist and dragged her to the ground with him.

"Damn it!" He groaned and wondered if she'd broken his nose. "Why you got a need to beat on me so goddamn hard?"

She struggled to get free.

He just kept an arm clamped around her waist, let her struggle all she wanted. He'd dropped his weapon when she'd rammed her head into his face, not a good thing for his training score, but when he'd fallen with her, he landed on the gun, a hard lump under his butt causing yet more pain he could blame on her. At least while he was sitting on it, she couldn't steal it.

With his other hand he tested his nose. He managed not to scream in pain, so he figured it wasn't broken. Not even bloody. Just hurting like hell.

"That's your new name," he told the woman who aimed an elbow at the charley-horse point on his thigh, the same move he'd just used on her to get free of the headlock.

She missed, thank God. Woman had sharp elbows he knew from experience.

"Agent Beat Belfour."

Finally realizing that he had her and her only way out would be to shoot him, she relaxed.

Once again he was captivated by the feel and smell of this woman. So much strength and power, but so soft and warm in his arms.

He'd thought of little else since the last time she'd beat the crap out of him up close and personal like this.

With a twist of his arm, he hauled her into his lap and kissed her.

For a long perfect moment, she leaned into the kiss. Hard and strong, just like the rest of her, and soft and warm as well. What was a heady scent on her skin, was a mule kick of flavor on his tongue.

He'd been wrong before. His nightly imagination, for those few moments he'd been awake before crashing into hammered-down sleep each night, had remembered her smelling of midnight and roses. True, her lips tasted of that, but beyond that her mouth was pure fire, lit up inside him so hot he burned.

Then she got him.

Finally landed that right hook square into his solar plexus. Then Beat Belfour was gone into the night.

Chapter 8

Frank: Now

Gone! *What the hell* do you mean she's gone?"

"Keep your voice down." Hank Henson had pulled him aside the moment that the President had entered his first conference with the U.N. Secretary-General. They stood fifteen feet from the Sec-Gen's door, thirty-eight stories up in the Secretariat Tower.

"We don't know much yet. You know where she was stationed?"

"Sure," and Frank felt sick. Beat had pulled escort duty on the ambassador to Senegal right at the westernmost bulge of Africa. The U.S. ambassador had been receiving death threats and the Secret Service had sent her to investigate the degree of danger. She was an expert on both West Africa and personal security, so the Secret Service had loaned her to the Office of Foreign Missions for a couple of weeks. That in itself was pretty normal, but—

"Agent Belfour…" Henson kept his hands up as if to fend off Frank's anger. Not a bad idea. Right at this moment Frank could understand the desire to kill the messenger.

"… was accompanying Ambassador Sam Green and three assistants, left Dakar yesterday, July first, at seven a.m. local time. They were headed to a series of meetings at Bissau in Guinea-Bissau. There's no ambassador there because we have no permanent diplomatic mission there."

"Because the place is such a goddamn hellhole they can't keep a government in place."

"Granted." Hank rolled right on with his whispered report that several of the closer secretaries were trying desperately to overhear. "It's only a one-hour flight. The locally-staffed liaison office called at five p.m. to ask if they'd left Dakar yet, they were eight hours overdue at that time. Then the locals went home because it was the end of the work day. When the Senegalese operator tried to confirm with Guinea-Bissau this morning, July second, they couldn't get a response at all, so they finally reported them late. The G-B liaison office is still not answering."

Frank needed to hit something and hit it hard.

The fine wood paneling smelled faintly of a recent lemon-oiling. The Sec-Gen's secretaries sat in a row of neatly aligned desks. Several elegant comfortable chairs were clustered in front of the thirty-eighth floor window, with its spectacular view of the Manhattan shoreline, to accommodate waiting dignitaries. Not a single Senegalese or Guinea-Bissau office worker to punch anywhere. Not even a padded wall in a sparring gym to pound on.

"Twenty-four hours?" was all he could grind out of his tight throat. They'd been missing for twenty-four hours before word had gotten back.

"No, Guinea-Bissau is ahead of us. In local time they are thirty hours overdue now."

"Someone just kill me now."

"You wouldn't like it." Hank's sense of humor never lurked far beneath the surface and gave Frank a tempting new target. "If I killed you, you wouldn't have a chance to pummel whoever screwed this up."

"Great. You're a big help." He paced to the Sec-Gen's office door and back. He allowed himself up to a max of twenty feet away before he considered himself off post. Typically a nation's guards waited in the comfortable chairs over fifty feet away, and watched the view of the Manhattan skyline. He was the United States Secret Service, Frank stayed close and watched the area around the door.

"We're having a hard time getting any communication in or out. We think they may be having another coup. It has been over a year since the last one, and we did just capture that rear admiral of theirs in the drug-and-arms-trafficking ring."

Frank couldn't shake the need to do something, anything, and he had only one option on that score.

"Keep me posted." Then he turned until he once again stood two steps to the right of the office door, behind which the President of the United States was in a meeting, and shifted into parade rest.

He scanned the room, everything and everyone where it had been two minutes before. Everything in place.

Except his world, which had now been turned upside down.

Chapter 9

Beatrice: 1988

B*eatrice sat in the* dark of the Georgia night, a hundred yards from the battered Ford Fairlane and the bleeding Frank Adams. She hadn't meant to bloody him, but that happened during training. Still, she hadn't meant to.

The heat scorching the Federal Law Enforcement Training Center had been at the front of her mind while she'd waited hidden in the back of the car.

Now she had a different heat to consider. And it wasn't one she liked. She didn't want to feel this way about anyone. Especially not some piece of crap off the street who had tried to carjack her. Except Frank Adams wasn't that. She knew more about him than she was supposed to, had managed to talk her way onto the background investigation team.

He lived with three other guys in a third-floor walk up. A Morningside Heights project at the far upper-west end of Manhattan. One so bad that it should never have been built to begin with, never mind torn down. When the investigating team went in, she was glad there were four agents together, the neighborhood was that rough.

They'd done round-robin interviews of all three of his roommates, each team member conducting their own individual interview. That way the Secret Service team could compare stories and answers afterward.

Big guy named Hale might have been the one to sit on her car hood. The build was right, but she'd only seen him from the back, and only briefly at that before Frank had blinded her windshield with his window-cleaning spray. She'd bet that the three roommates had all been around her car that night.

She didn't worry about that. Without Frank, they weren't likely to be more than petty criminals. What was interesting was that none of them would give up the least thing about Frank despite, she knew, Frank telling them it was okay. Their various stories about him were somewhat inconsistent, just as always happened in real life unless you practiced the stories, but they were totally loyal to him. She'd pushed hard on the carjacking, without mentioning that to the other agents or in her reports.

She hit a stone wall, even after saying she'd been the woman in the car and recognized each of them. These guys would lie their way right into jail to protect Frank. He'd earned absolute loyalty in a world that didn't trade in it.

Only child of a coke whore who'd been dead half a decade. Apparently she'd tried to be a good mother despite that. Father, no one had a clue. Even Frank had simply put a question mark on his background form. Hospital records had no other information. No one in his Morningside Heights project recalled a steady boyfriend for her, especially not from twenty years ago. Memories were short in the projects. But they'd remembered his mother as a lost soul, though pleasant and seriously pretty, right up to the overdose. Those were never pretty.

School teachers were deeply frustrated by him. Intelligent. Good grades. Didn't talk much, but had shown up consistently, a rarity in itself, and was never found without a thoughtful answer when questioned. The only telling remark she found was from a junior year science teacher. "Boy has no real focus on what to do with himself."

Beatrice sat with her back against one of the concrete barriers of the Georgia training grounds. Despite the night's heat, she pulled a dark hood over her head until it hung just above her eyes, masked to near invisibility like a Jawa. She wondered if Frank had ever seen *Star Wars*.

She wondered entirely too much about Frank for her own comfort. She'd discovered and shepherded him through application and recruiting, then dumped him into the training system. It should have ended there.

But her world hadn't returned to center. If it had, then what was she doing squatting in the cicada-throbbing darkness of FLETC with a knot on her head where she'd been shoved against the car door? Who knew the guy was so damn strong that he could stop a two-footed kick against the door with the palm of his hand. Her thigh still twinged where he'd dug his fingers into the nerve cluster to break a perfectly good headlock. And her lips still burned with the heat of his kiss.

She needed to put some real distance been them.

Then why are you sitting in the dark watching Frank Adams continue the exercise, Beatrice? You are so not going to be caught mooning over some man. You got away. You've got a role to play. Move your ass.

That the last order to herself sounded more like something Frank would say than herself, well, that only added to the problem. She kept an eye on his dark silhouette against the white Fairlane as she started moving sideways into the night.

Frank prowled the perimeter, his empty weapon drawn, aimed low, and swinging slowly before him exactly per training so that it was already in motion if he had to aim. It was faster to change direction of an active motion, than break muscle lock of a position held still for too long.

He hadn't sprinted after her.

Again, team player. It was a two-man exercise, and he didn't leave his partner with the unknown variable of the driver in the car. Any trainee that did was marked instantly dead by the trainers.

Actually, he wasn't moving quite per training. He was spending the bulk of his time on the side of the test zone that she'd exited from. Still looking for her.

He froze, his massive frame silhouetted by the flashlight his partner was using to inspect the vehicle. Frank was looking straight at her, or at least it felt like that. There was no way he could see her. No way he could know she'd begun to circle around and hadn't simply kept going.

But still he stood facing her, as if he could sense her even if he couldn't see where she stood a hundred feet into the brush.

Then he put one hand to his lips and ran it across his mouth. As if his lips also burned.

# # #

"Frank."

"Yo," he didn't turn at Jake Hellman's call. He could feel her out there. Over by the concrete barriers, that's where he'd bet Beat would go. At least to start, but then she'd move… that way… left. She'd be nothing but a shadow of a shadow, but he knew she was there. That kiss wouldn't

have let her just run. There'd been more than heat, more than his need…
or hers. It was as if they understood each other.

"Frank. She's gone."

"Right, sorry." He turned and blinked against the ghoulish brightness
of Jake's red-lensed flashlight. They said that red didn't mess with your
night vision. It did, just not as much. He'd felt, against all reason, that
another thirty seconds and he'd have been able to see Beat, nickname
definitely worked, out there in the darkness.

The Ford Fairlane sat on the empty dirt road. All of the doors wide
open, and the dome light now definitely shot his night vision all to hell.

He ran the scenario through his head again. They'd stopped the
car with a log dragged across the road, improvised road block. Driver
had pretended to not understand what was going on, only speaking in
something that might have been Czech or maybe just gibberish. The
person-of-interest role played by Agent Belfour hiding on the floor of
the back seat.

But she hadn't acted like a victim. No, she'd acted like a bodyguard.
The hidden asset.

"Jake, where's the driver?"

"I've got him tied up on the other side. All nerves."

"It's a switch-out. He's the target, she's the guard."

"You sure?" But even as Jake asked, he raced around the hood of the
car while Frank circled behind the trunk.

The driver was gone.

No. He wasn't. He'd rolled into a roadside ditch, hidden himself.
Given away by his white shirt and light-colored khakis.

Wait. Not hidden. He'd gotten himself low.

Frank dove at Jake and tackled him down into the ditch on top of the
driver just as a flashbang went off under the car, simulating an explosion
that would have blinded them for several minutes as well as labeling
them both as severely wounded if they were outside a fifteen foot radius,
dead if they were inside it.

Simulated car bomb.

The Fairlane still rested in the middle of the lane instead of being
blown into a thousand bits of shrapnel.

Before the light of the flashbang had fully faded, Frank had the
driver up on his knees beside the ditch, and placed the barrel of his
empty sidearm up against the man's temple. He held the man around the
chest, pulling him close like a shield.

He put his back to the car to ensure he made the smallest target possible.

"You okay, Jake?"

"Mostly." Jake's head and sidearm popped up out of the ditch for a second, then ducked back. "You ever play football?"

"Nose tackle."

"Uh, I can tell." Jake's head popped up where he'd crawled fifteen feet farther down the ditch and he scanned the trees.

Closest Frank had ever gotten to football was the big screen at Slade's Bar. But the Hispanic gangs of the Upper East Side were nasty in a street fight and Frank had learned that the best defense was indeed a good offense. Hammer them to the ground before they could respond.

But he'd more recently learned to keep that part of his past hidden. People didn't want to know about his street background. Most agents in the various training scenarios wanted to think their partners could've gone All-American, rather than gone lifetime sentence for manslaughter.

The driver, still wrapped in Frank's grip, flinched hard and looked down at his chest. Then he spoke his first clear words of the evening, "Oh shit!"

Three splotches of red oozed down his chest. He'd been shot from somewhere in the dark woods on the far side of the ditch. Three shots so fast, that he'd never stood a chance.

"Hate it when I'm sacrificed."

"Shut up, you're dead." The smell of fresh paint stung Frank's nose, almost making him sneeze.

"Don't I just know it." The paintball pellets must have stung through the driver-agent's light cotton shirt. Frank could feel the man shrug, then fall limp in his arms.

That's when Frank made the mistake of letting him slide to the ground.

Knowing instantly that he'd screwed up, Frank dove to the right, but was too late.

A line of paintball shots stitched across his own chest.

He lay on the ground, technically bleeding out, as Agent Beatrice Ann Belfour slid out of the trees.

"Bang! You're dead."

Chapter 10

Frank: Now

Can we at least confirm if she's dead or not?" Frank trusted to his instincts to watch the Secretary-General's outer office and yet allow his mind concentrate on the information coming in.

"Maybe the ambassador too?" He knew Hank was teasing him over the encrypted two-way radio link, but he couldn't organize his thoughts enough to care about Ambassador Sam Green at the moment.

"Sure," Frank conceded begrudgingly. "But I can guarantee that if Beat is alive, then so is the ambassador." No question that she'd be down before whoever she was protecting.

Hank had radioed on a private frequency that went straight to Frank rather than the open channel to the whole PPD team. Hank was in the U.S. security office down in the U.N. basement.

"Only thing I can confirm is that another coup is going on. The French Embassy has told us that everyone is shut down and waiting for the next government to be installed."

"There's a joke for you."

"Yeah," Hank agreed. No trace of humor in him this time.

There'd been no need to explain the joke. "Government" was not something Guinea-Bissau had experienced much of lately. For a decade, G-B had been a narco-state. Coups were frequent and bloody. In 2009, the on-again, off-again President, the only one considered even close to decent, was gunned down in revenge for assassinating the head of his joint chiefs of staff. Of course, he'd had the supreme military commander killed for attempting a coup. And so it went on. In 2012, the latest military ruler had disbanded parliament as a "cost savings measure." The country had the lowest standard of living in the world, which was really saying something. Something awful.

Now it sounded as if the Acting President would be next under the gun, after having his two opponents arrested when he'd lost an election against them. Cocaine shifted across the G-B borders in multi-ton quantities, enroute to Europe or the U.S. Just a few months ago, the former head of their navy had been caught transshipping eleven hundred kilograms of cocaine and enough surface-to-air missiles to make a real mess of the DEA helicopters flying in Colombia.

"Any idea who is ousting who?"

"No. The last three coups have all been military factions in-fighting for control of the drug trade, so your guess is as good as mine. They always kill off a few top politicians along the way."

"When can the French Embassy get someone on the ground?"

"Their best estimate is five to seven days based on prior upheavals, though they said the worst coup required two weeks. Until then, they're keeping their people locked down. Russia was able to evacuate their people last night, along with Belgium and Germany. Assets in the country are real thin."

"Shit!" Frank let go of the frequency and glared at the secretaries who had turned to look at him. They saw his hot glare and abruptly found work to do on their desks.

The door beside Frank opened and the President strode out of the Secretary-General's office.

"Everything okay here, Frank?"

"Yes sir, Mr. President." There'd be a briefing ready within the hour, but there was no point in distracting the President with incomplete information before that time.

Chapter 11

Beatrice: 1988

The key, people," *Beat* stood at the front of the training center lecture room. "The key is learning to act accurately and quickly on incomplete information." Two dozen agent-wannabes slumped in their seats, well past exhaustion. The room was a double-wide trailer, shabby from a hundred training classes and thousands of post-action analyses. The Georgia heat was so concentrated in here that she was surprised the plastic carpet didn't melt.

"Most of you pre-judged the roles. Make no assumptions. Ever!" She put a slide up on the screen. "Lynette Alice 'Squeaky' Fromme assassination attempt on President Ford during which no shots were fired." Click-clack of the advancing slide. "Sarah Jane Moore repeated the attempt seventeen days later, actually firing her weapon and wounding a nearby taxi driver." Click-clack. "Mark David Chapman who had John Lennon sign an album, then gunned him down six hours later." Click-clack. "Two months after that John Hinckley, Jr. succeeded in seriously wounding President Reagan in an effort to impress Jodi Foster who he was stalking. She was eighteen at the time."

Beatrice click-clacked through another dozen slides, all types of would-be and successful assassins operating on U.S. soil, and not a one looked demented or stereotypically terrorist. The slide projector clicking and the hum of the air conditioner that failed to fight back the heat or the body odor of the twenty men and four women struggling to stay awake in their chairs, were the only other sounds in the room.

"Only one of you recognized the driver was the target of the scenario." There was no need to point out who, the three paintball stains across Frank's chest had dried dark red on his shirt and were there for all to see.

"However," Beatrice pointed out before he could start to be too pleased with himself. "He made the false assumption that the companions of the person-of-interest would think him important enough to keep alive. Instead, they decided to sacrifice him to keep him from being questioned, which was the stated top criteria of the exercise. Most of you were killed by the simulated car bomb, he was killed by three bullets to the chest, and critical information on a terrorist plot was lost with the driver's death in all cases. Never assume."

She waited in silence, staring at the room in general and carefully not looking at Frank's hurt expression. That he'd gotten the highest score from observers by a factor of two was beside the point, and one she wouldn't be mentioning. She'd also be keeping silent about Frank being the only trainee to take her down, even briefly.

She didn't invite questions, that wasn't the point. She wanted to drive, to "beat" the point home. Damn him. That nickname had already begun to run through the other trainers. It was better than her childhood nickname of Beebee, for Beatrice Belfour, but not much. She'd had to pound that one into the ground throughout grade school, but the more she attempted to bury "Beat" the more often it cropped up. She had a nasty feeling this one was going to run through the agency.

"Dismissed. Get clean and get some sleep." After three months of FLETC they knew that they wouldn't have time to catch up on sleep. Drills at odd hours, functioning on high alert for days in crisis situations, learning to fight through the time when hallucinations from lack of sleep set in.

She waited until they were all gone, then shut down the projector and the lights.

He was waiting for her in the midnight shadows, leaning back against one of the trees of the low forest cultured for use in these scenarios.

Of course, he was. As she'd known he'd be.

She stood under the small yellow porch light of the double-wide, four steel steps to the ground.

He didn't move, leaving the choice to her.

Her boyfriend in college had not understood her sophomore-year turn from art, originally chosen to piss off her parents, to criminology, chosen to please herself.

Once she'd signed up for agent training, she only seemed to attract the men who were interested in proving they could out-wrestle a Secret Service agent. None of their egos had taken kindly to her definitive proof that none of them could.

Frank Adams was the first man in a long time who hadn't seen her as a target, something to conquer. Instead he waited and watched as her blood burned in the hot Georgia night and her pulse raced.

She was barely conscious of the steps she descended or the rough ground she crossed until they stood just inches apart under the trees. The night air scented by the tiny white flowers of the glorybower tree, punch strong but with a sweetness as soft as a truly fine gelato on a hot summer night. The blooms looked like stars lost from the sky and scattered over the dark green leaves, the only light in the darkness.

"Last time you socked me in the gut," his voice was a gentle rumble in the shadows.

She had.

"Good punch by the way." He slid his hands around her waist.

"Thanks," she wrapped her own around his neck.

He nuzzled her hair, "Even hot and sweaty you smell amazing."

She let herself lean her cheek against his chest and breathe him in. "So do you."

He scooped her up into his arms as if she were a feather. "Now's the time to say it if you're going to."

She kept her mouth shut, her arms around his neck, and her cheek on his chest.

He waited three heartbeats that she could feel and hear in his chest, then he strode into the woods until she wondered how he navigated at all. Even the tiny five-petal flowers faded away, though not their glorious scent that wrapped about them like a protective shawl.

He didn't set her down to kiss her, but simply kept her cradled against him. His mouth impossibly soft, his arms incredibly strong.

Beatrice had fought against everything in her life: her nicknames, her parents, the system, even the training rules. In Frank's arms, there was no need to fight at all. His kiss was everything she hadn't expected from the man she'd swept off the street three months ago. It was soft, playful, and included a smile when they finally moaned in unison.

He set her on her feet and leaned her back against a tree. He pinned her there with his lips, with the gentle brushstrokes of those big hands. He knelt before her and feasted on her body, and all she could do was hold on. When at last he had her naked against the tree, she guided him over her. A willing lover, one who made her feel things she hadn't felt before.

Not just the amazing rocketing sensations firing through her body in unprecedented waves of heat and pleasure. Not simply desired either. He made her feel needed. Important. As if being here with her was the only thing he cared about in the world.

When he had shed his own clothes and leaned naked upon her, skin-to-skin, she didn't go wild as she'd thought she'd might, ravenous for his touch and smell. Instead a peace settled over her as she traced her hands over his beautiful chest, invisible in the darkness, but still beautiful.

"Been thinking about this, haven't you?" she whispered when he reached down to his pants and pulled out some protection with a soft crackle of foil.

"Since the moment you pulled that damn gun on me."

"A gun turns you on?" She teased his pecs with her tongue.

"No." His groan rippled against her lips. "A gun makes my balls shrivel in fear."

She laughed and rested her forehead against his sternum as he stroked his hands up and down her back.

"But the woman who was wielding it turned me on since before I even heard her name."

"Damn you," her soft curse was lost against his lips as he lifted her by cupping his strong hands into a seat as she wrapped her legs about his hips.

He leaned her back against the tree and took her, one of the most incredible experiences of her twenty-three years.

"You feel even better than my car."

His chuckle was deep and rippled along her chest.

"Damn high praise that."

Chapter 12

S he's the best."

Frank knew better than to feel offended. First, the President was trying to make him feel better in a potentially ugly situation. Second, he was absolutely right. Even he wasn't as good as Agent Beatrice Belfour.

He needed to remember that.

If anyone could get out of this alive, it was Beat.

"So, what's the situation?"

Hank had radioed Frank that they were ready to brief the President on the G-B situation. Frank had informed the President as he came out of a quick meeting with the European Central Bank representative to the U.N., checking in on the latest banking crisis to hit the European Union. All of the aftershocks of the American recession were still having brutal ripple effects around the world. The recovery ripples just now crossing America were still a year or more in the future for Europe and Asia.

When Frank told the President about the problem in Guinea-Bissau, he'd immediately rescheduled a coffee chat with India and they'd taken the elevator down to the Secret Service's security office in the basement.

"I don't know the situation yet, Mr. President." Frank stuck his head out of the elevator and looked carefully both ways despite being inside the U.N. security perimeter. Two of his agents at either end of the hall signaled clear.

Frank led the President across the hall and down two doors. "I just know that she and the ambassador have been missing for thirty-one hours now. I'm hoping we've found out more than that." And if they hadn't, he just might steal a plane and fly over there himself to see what he could find out.

He went through the first door and inspected the small outer room. Six feet square, it had an American flag, a steel door, and a camera.

Once the outer door had latched behind them, two sharp buzzes filled the room. The first, driving bolts into the door behind them. The second, releasing the bolts on the door ahead. They moved into the war room.

A line of agents sat at terminals along the right-hand wall. They were responsible for the security of the room, coordinating all U.S. agent activities within the U.N. complex, and controlling outside security. Along the left wall a series of stations faced inward, about a third of these were staffed. They were responsible for communications, research, and anything needed by the active teams on site, including the U.S. Ambassador to the U.N., presently in London.

In the center, a table that could seat ten faced a trio of large flat screens on the far wall.

The room wasn't as secure and flexible as the White House Situation Room, but it was close. Close enough to observe and address world crises. Frank glared at the G-B map presently filling the central screen. Especially in unstable little ratholes like Guinea-Bissau.

The President joined Hank at the table, Frank stood behind a swivel chair and held on until his fingers ached where they dug into the leather. But he couldn't let go.

It was Hank's briefing. Frank had retasked him to prepare this briefing because, despite his constant joking and deep joy in hazing rookies, he was a top agent. No military commander could get to New York, cleared into the U.N.'s extraterritorial zone, and be sufficiently briefed in time, so Frank had loaned Hank to them as a liaison. If the situation escalated, they could call the Joint Chiefs into the Situation Room and link down to them.

At least with Hank on the case, Frank could stay focused on the President's security.

Mostly.

"We've been able to confirm that the ambassador's plane landed in Bissau at Osvaldo Vieira International. Thankfully we had the Nimitz-class aircraft carrier *Harry S. Truman* in the vicinity. They flew a Raptor drone overhead twenty minutes ago and were able to identify the plane."

A slide came up of the one-strip airport. A white circle around a tiny white cross on gray tarmac. The next slide a close-up so good he could almost count the rivets of the embassy's Beech King Air.

There was a dark blotch on the tarmac at the foot of the steps. A blotch that didn't look like spilled oil. Hank didn't comment on it, so neither did Frank. They'd both seen the spray and bleed-out pattern of a single headshot before. It wasn't important to the tactical situation, other than to confirm it sucked. They already knew that, without the confirmation. No body in evidence, no way to tell anything about who it had been.

The President's skin, gone abruptly gray, told that he'd reached the same conclusion.

Hank put up the next slide. It showed a small building, or rather the remains of one.

The walls had been blown out sideways, the roof was gone. Inside were the remains of a pair of SUVs. A close-up revealed a leg and an arm, the first stuck out from beneath a section of the roof, the other wasn't attached to anything.

The silence in the room was so thick that it pressed in on Frank from every side. Everyone was waiting for his reaction and he wasn't ready to have one yet.

"Do we have a higher resolution image?"

Hank said something to one of the left-wall techs and the image jumped inward until the two body parts were nearly life-size projected against the wall. So close you could smell the red dust, the black char from the fire, and the deep-in-the-throat bite of copper that was spilled blood.

The arm wore a golden bracelet, not something Beat would ever wear in the field.

The leg had a men's shoe.

He swallowed hard and managed to keep his voice steady.

"What else do we know?"

# # #

"What we know," Beat turned to face Ambassador Green. "Is that we need to remain calm and quiet."

"But…"

She held up a hand to silence him.

Okay, she hadn't killed the man, yet. Though she was certainly going to reserve that option. He still survived mostly because it was bad form to kill the man you were sworn to protect. And a little bit because he was such a fish out of water that she had to pity him. He'd been a political appointee by the prior administration rather than a career diplomat. And that he'd been assigned to the Senegalese embassy only said how low he was on the totem pole. He should have contributed more to the last President's campaign, or to a different party and stayed in Kansas or wherever he hailed from.

Three years he'd been in Senegal and he had the common sense of a hamster. For one thing, after seeing what he'd signed up for, he'd stayed. Bad choice right out of the gate. This would be a hard posting even for a career Foreign Service diplomat. At least he appeared to be trying to do the right thing, but he really needed to learn to listen to direction.

Of course his *chief attaché* was currently lying in little pieces along with the remains of the embassy's two SUVs and airport garage. Up until the explosion, those vehicles and a small liaison office downtown had been the sole assets of the U.S. government in Guinea-Bissau. Now only the office remained.

When the explosion occurred, she and the ambassador had been waiting halfway to the garage while his assistant trotted back to the plane on her mid-heel pumps for his forgotten briefcase. The *chief attaché* and the *chargé d'affaires* hadn't been so fortunate. They'd gone ahead to the garage, a fancy word for a concrete block with two metal roll-up doors she could have unlocked in less than a minute without keys or explosives.

After much hiding, and three miles of sneaking through the suburbs of a city at war, the airport now lay thirty hours behind them. In their weaving track, they'd covered perhaps a quarter of that distance from the airport as the crow flies.

They huddled now in a hut of cracked, sun-baked brick walls and a rotting tin roof. The red dirt floor bore little in the way of debris or belongings, indicating that it was, perhaps, if their luck was changing even a little please, vacant. She'd erased their footprints for a hundred paces back, but they had to stay quiet and out of sight.

The ambassador and Charlotte his personal secretary, clearly with side benefits, huddled hip to hip against the back wall. Whatever they did on the side wasn't her business, neither wore a ring anyway. They were swathed as she was, in clothing snagged from clotheslines.

Sam Green's black pants with a simple white *dashiki* hanging to mid-calf over them worked well. She had him scuff up his black dress shoes. If anything had driven home the reality of their situation for him, even more than witnessing the explosion that had killed his two top-ranked staffers, it was when she'd grabbed the shoe from his hands as he gently patted it with red dirt. Beatrice had scrubbed it against some broken concrete until it was deeply scarred, then shoved it into the soil and handed it back to him.

Charlotte actually looked quite fetching in the traditional golden yellow-and-brown print *buba* and wrap-around sarong skirt. Beatrice had snagged a traditional head wrap for her, but Charlotte couldn't keep it on her long, smooth hair. Even the head scarf kept slipping down around her shoulders.

Beatrice herself had found a bright blue *pagne* blouse and matching skirt. It would have been garish or at least stand-out in any environ other than West Africa, but here it blended in.

Charlotte's feet weren't up to running barefoot, so she'd retained the bright blue pumps that didn't fit in at all. Of course, neither did her or Green's blond hair, blue eyes, and New England-fair skin. They'd be a beautiful couple in a Boston townhouse, but they sure didn't belong on the streets of an African country on the verge of collapse.

And neither of them knew how to move. She'd tried to show them the lazy, ambling walk of sub-Saharan equatorial Africa. That had been a fiasco. It was as if they'd traveled direct from prep school to an alien planet and learned nothing during their time in Africa. Charlotte was doing better than the ambassador, but not much. No matter how nice they might be as people or how good they might be at diplomacy, they were lost causes when it came to hiding out and blending in.

The three of them had been barely a dozen yards from the garage when it went up. She'd seen the fizzle of a failed explosive device and thrown the ambassador and Charlotte behind the next garage over just as the backup device blew the world to shit.

She'd turned to sprint them back to the plane, hoping she could find some way to fly it out of there before someone shot it down. Then she'd spotted the army jeep roaring up beside it just in time to duck back out of sight. A ragtag trio climbed aboard the Beech King Air, their Soviet-era Kalashnikov machine guns leading the way. They hauled the Senegalese pilot out of the plane. Only Beat's hand over Charlotte's mouth had stopped the scream when they'd executed him on the tarmac beside the embassy plane.

Beatrice had dragged them to their feet and actually hit and slapped them until they started running.

Now, thirty hours later, they huddled in the midday heat. Her throat aching with the dry dust and blazing equatorial heat.

Their assets included her handgun, four spare magazines, one briefcase full of paperwork and a few pens that the ambassador had refused to abandon, but she'd gotten him to stuff it into a stolen burlap sack he'd then carried over his shoulder, and a pair of blue pumps. No cell phone signals, and the neighborhoods they'd passed through had no overhead lines, so no electricity or landline phones.

The shocking number of tacticals, white Toyota pickups with .50 caliber machine guns turreted in their beds, did not point to finding much help in the city.

Still, she'd listened initially to Ambassador Green's insistence on reaching the American Liaison Office or the Presidential Palace in the heart of the city. But the black smoke now rising from that direction indicated that this time, if it was again a coup, it had not gone as smoothly as the prior executions of a few key leaders. Thirty hours of hard work and they'd covered less than two of the six kilometers to the city center. And the chances of survival decreased with every meter in that direction.

After dark, she'd see if the people around here had any food to steal.

And maybe someone had a pair of sandals for Charlotte.

#

"Is the Guinea-Bissau ambassador to the U.N. here today? Ambassador Anselmo?"

Frank looked at the President in shock. Why the hell hadn't he thought of that? And how had the President remembered the guy's name? He was always doing that, as if his brain operated on a whole different level.

Frank hadn't thought of it because they barely have a government was his answer. But anything was worth a shot.

One of the techs rattled her keyboard, "Yes."

"Extension?" Hank called out and dialed it on the central table's speaker phone even as she dictated it.

In minutes they had an appointment.

Frank could definitely appreciate traveling with the President. The man got things done.

Chapter 13

Frank: 1988

N*o way in hell* that this is done." Three months they'd been sleeping together on the sly. Three months and the heat, smell, taste of Beatrice Ann Belfour was burned right into Frank's nerve endings.

They sat on the bench where they'd perched a lifetime and six months ago. This time it was late morning rather than two a.m. And it was frickin' January-butt-clench cold. But everything else was much the same.

The Brooklyn Bridge soared above them, the restaurant and its lousy fake security cameras was doing a lively business despite the frigid winter morning. The East River Ferry slid into DUMBO dock. He kept meaning to look up why they called it that, but never had. A glance over his shoulder and he could see by the giant clock atop the Watchtower building that the boat was running ten minutes late as usual.

They were sitting right where the old man had howled at the moon along with his dogs in *Moonstruck*. He almost smiled at the memory of the frantic love they'd made after watching it, right down to the full moonlight streaming into his Brooklyn studio apartment window. Still a third-floor walkup, but the tiny apartment in the brownstone owned by a couple of artists was a hell of a lot better than the Morningside Heights projects.

He finally forced himself to look down at Agent Beatrice Ann Belfour sitting beside him on the cold metal. Her dark hair was tucked under a knit hat of blue and green stripes. Her red parka was zipped so far up her neck that her face almost disappeared into it. It made her appear about twice her true size. He could appreciate that, as his sweatshirt and jacket were not up to the task of keeping him warm even with the hoodie up. But her words had sent a much greater chill coursing down his spine.

"We have to be done. We're fraternizing."

"I'm not the goddamn enemy." He knew his anger wasn't helping, but he was way past being able to control that.

"I'm a full agent, you're a trainee. I can't keep putting that at risk for me and I can't put that at risk for you."

"Like I could give a rat's ass." Though he actually did, which was kinda weird. He wanted this to work, a whole life beyond the projects that he'd never imagined. But he wanted her more.

She wasn't looking at him.

That's what was killing him. Those dark, fathomless eyes were glazed over and facing off somewhere in the direction of Manhattan, not at him. Not making him feel warm inside. Instead, they froze him out.

"My next assignment arrived this morning."

"And you didn't tell me?" His shout was loud enough that some of the passengers debarking from the East River ferry stumbled on the gangplank in the hurry to look in his direction and just as quickly away.

"I'm telling you now."

She was. Damn it! He bit his tongue.

"I'm telling you first."

Double damn! For six months he'd kept his temper in check. Once the trainers had learned he could control that, they'd pounded on him, trying to get a rise, trying to find out just how deep his control ran. It had gotten so deep that some of the other trainees had gotten mad on his behalf and stepped in the way of the obvious hazing. He'd kept his cool, except around Beat.

He couldn't do it now when he needed it. Not with Beatrice telling him they were done. He closed his eyes, took a deep breath.

"Okay." Another. "What is it?"

"I'm going to be working Africa for the next six months. Traveling station to station, verifying and standardizing Secret Service security operations and interface with local agencies. It's a great oppor—"

"And now you're telling me that you're going to take it no matter what I say." Frank had been prepared to ride out whatever she'd be doing. But not this. Not six months of it. That he couldn't figure how to swallow.

She didn't look at him, not even after the ferry reloaded and moved on across the shining water.

Finally she nodded, then hung her head.

Beatrice Belfour never hung her head.

Think, Frank. You've always let her do the thinking. Time you tried some of that. She's the one who pulled you out of the shit projects and the hard-time future. She risked her career and shared her body. She was the one he was totally gone on. What have you risked?

Nothing!

And she never mentioned her family. He'd only met them once, totally by accident when they spotted her car and flagged her down. New York was weird like that. You could be way out of your normal 'hood and you'd run into a friend on the street you hadn't seen in six months, despite knowin' you lived just three blocks apart.

Family wasn't a place he bothered to think of much. But it had been real damn clear that her folks weren't expecting no Frank Adams.

That must hurt like hell too. She'd given everything and he'd just been cruisin' along for the ride, not giving it any thought.

Well, it was time to start doing that.

"Okay," he breathed deep until the cold air pierced his insides like frozen needles. "Okay." He turned to face her.

She didn't look up.

Thinking it better not to cup her chin and turn her face, he pressed a finger against her hunched shoulder, slowly turning her toward him and forcing her shoulder back until she looked up.

"I'll wait."

"But—"

"I'll wait!" He cut her off harshly. Knew he was being a jerk, not letting her finish her thoughts. But he had to make the point so she heard it.

She stared at him for a long time, those dark eyes boring into him, seeking some truth he'd never find.

Finally, that single nod.

What the hell was that anyway? Frank Adams didn't wait for any woman.

Beatrice got up and walked back toward her car to head into the New York office of the United States freaking Secret Service.

Frank stayed and blinked against the cold sunlight burning his eyes.

For Beatrice Ann Belfour, he'd damn sure wait.

Chapter 14

Frank: Now

No, we need answers right now, Ambassador Anselmo." The President was not in one of his patient moods. "What is happening in your country, in Guinea-Bissau, right now?"

"Nothing is bad happening in my country. Can assure your nation of that, President Matthews."

Frank wanted to pound his fist into the man's dark face and then his ever so bright diplomat's smile wouldn't look so pretty. And by the time he was done, the man's Brooks Brothers' pinstripe would also be seriously mussed.

They sat in the Guinea-Bissau ambassador's office in the U.N. Secretariat Tower. It had none of the grandeur of the U.N. Secretary-General's. A lone receptionist, a pretty woman in a traditional red blouse, sarong, and sandaled feet, had greeted them kindly. Clearly one of the highlights of her day, not just meeting the American President, but meeting anyone in this quiet corner of the floor where the West African nations were clustered together. Her desk had been clearly devoid of any work, despite the ambassador's presence.

Anselmo's office bore little of the traditional African décor. Instead he had drawn deeply on the designs, colors, and motifs of his country's heritage as a former Portuguese colony. Frank felt like he'd been trapped in an Iberian version of a Pottery Barn store. Nothing felt authentic.

"Then perhaps you can explain the attack on my embassy aircraft," the President's voice was calm. Matter of fact.

Hank Henson set down the photo of the massive bloodstain by the airplane's exit stairs as the President spoke.

Frank had heard the President angry before, but this wasn't angry. This was something new. He'd gone very quiet, so soft-spoken that Frank could barely hear him though he stood only two steps behind his chair. This was dangerous. In two years of serving with him, and six months on the campaign trail before that, he'd never heard that tone from Peter Matthews.

"After that would you care to explain the deaths of my embassy personnel?"

The photo of the exploded garage landed on the ambassador's broad and empty desk, next to a gruesome close-up of the body parts, still there thirty-two hours later.

"The torching of my liaison office."

A photo of the smoke still smoldering around the remains of the U.S. Liaison office building in downtown Bissau.

"These are acts of war, Mr. Ambassador. You have one hour to produce answers. After that, I will make any decisions I deem appropriate to determine the security of my remaining personnel on the ground."

The President stood and moved from the room so quickly that Frank was hard pressed to stay in front of him. Hank brought up the rear.

As soon as they were in the elevator, the President began speaking quickly.

"You saw his face. He doesn't know anything is wrong. Completely out of the loop, he's playing the game with a tray full of vowels. I'll wager he can't even communicate with anyone in G-B at this time, though I'm sure he is only at this very instant discovering that."

Frank blinked, it took him only that long to catch up with the President's thoughts.

"Then why did you give him an hour?" Frank wouldn't have given him thirty seconds.

The President didn't answer, instead he turned to Hank as the elevator continued downward.

"Hank, what's our closest asset? The *Harry S. Truman* where they launched the Raptor drone?"

"Good memory, yes sir. Operation Sure Seas off Nigeria. Nigeria's trying to outdo Somalia on being the terror of ocean-shipping channels. The *Truman*'s leading a task group to fight them back."

"Find out how fast they can have assets into Guinea-Bissau. Get the Joint Chiefs involved. We aren't waiting an hour, we aren't waiting a minute, I just wanted to give their ambassador some motivation. I do wish I hadn't mentioned surviving U.S. citizens on the ground."

In retrospect, Frank agreed. If the ambassador could get through to whatever was the government of the moment, he would tell them there was someone they needed to find. The question was whether it would be to find and save, or find and silence.

At the basement floor Hank got off the elevator, but the President remained, so Frank stayed with him. The President held the door as he finished passing instructions to Hank.

"I have a luncheon with Russia, a meeting with Pakistan that isn't going to be any fun at all, and a dinner with Great Britain and France. After dinner there's an informal but essential meeting with Laos, Cambodia, and Vietnam about a combined trade agreement. I can't delay any of those, but I'll run things through Frank. Keep him posted. Call Daniel at the White House. Tell my Chief of Staff to get his wife on this and to get everyone in the Sit Room. I'll deal with the attacks on U.S. property and personnel later. I want our people in Guinea-Bissau found and found now."

He let the elevator door close without completing the statement to Hank, which Frank appreciated. He didn't need to hear the President of the United States say about Beatrice Belfour, "if there is anyone still alive to be found."

Once again, he was stuck with waiting.

#

"What we need at the moment is patience. You have to stay here."

Ambassador Sam Green and Charlotte looked at Beatrice as if she'd gone mad. Well, that wouldn't surprise her much at the moment. Trapped with the two of them in a narco-state undergoing a coup wasn't exactly a rational experience. Guinea-Bissau didn't have a large number of motor vehicles, and most of those were ancient motor scooters.

Yet, through the cracks in the wall of the hut they were hiding in, the roads were far from empty. They were hiding in a warren of ramshackle huts southeast of the airport, but one that afforded her a narrow view of the one main street in the whole city. In the last few hours squatting here, she'd seen a dozen tacticals, the white Toyota pickups just bristling with armed and angry militia, and two tanks that looked to be left over from when the place had gained independence in the '70s. She knew they had about thirty tanks, but intelligence had been unsure how many actually worked and how many of those had shells for their main cannon. She could hear something pounding away in the city center, clearly someone had some ammunition. The place was really coming apart. Again. She even spotted one of their two known helicopters.

"You have to stay put here," she pointed emphatically at the hut's dirt floor.

"Not alone. We can't."

Beatrice was never prepared for this stage of working protection jobs. The moment when the protectee turned into, what the department carefully didn't call, "the sniveling child" phase. Young children never dared circulate far from their parents. Protectees would latch onto their bodyguard's metaphorical skirts and become a real pain.

Technically, it was called a stage-two trauma response.

Beatrice sighed. At least they were finally out of the stage-one denial. Now the ambassador had apparently opted for fear and confusion in stage two. She could do with the help from anger, but he hadn't gone there. The Secret Service had trained her how to shift in mere seconds from precipitating event to stage three, new equilibrium. Only from equilibrium could the decision-making process accurately resume.

If she could do a Vulcan mind-meld and shift Sam Green forward through the stages, she would. Though she seriously doubted she'd like what else she learned about him during the meld.

Charlotte had moved on to anger. Apparently she and the now dead *chargé d'affaires* had been shopping buddies. That would be helpful, so she addressed Charlotte.

"Look, if you want to get out of this alive so you can work on fixing this place so this never happens again…" Fat chance of that. Guinea-Bissau would be cycling through hell for decades to come just as it had for the last half century. These kinds of places always did. "… Then I need you to stay here and stay quiet. I'm going to get food and water. I'm also going to try and scout our way out of here."

Charlotte's sharp nod of agreement confirmed that the woman's brain had kicked back in. And that she was really looking forward to kicking some serious butt to revenge the *chargé d'affaire's* death.

Beatrice momentarily considered handing over her gun, but decided against it. The last thing she needed was for Sam Green to suddenly take it from his more rational assistant and decide he was G.I. Joe. Or, more likely, to go out and think that he could talk sense to these people at gunpoint.

Instead, she told Charlotte. "Don't let him leave. There's half a million people here. If I lose you, you're going to be dead."

"And if we stay with you?" She saw in his eyes that Ambassador Green was at least part way back.

Beatrice shrugged. "Then I'll see what I can do to improve our chances."

#

For three hours Beatrice prowled the streets of Bissau. Starting her scouting in late evening, blending smoothly among what people there were along the street, darkness descended with that sudden slice-of-a-knife abruptness typical of tropical countries. The moonlight, and the warm glow of cooking fires lit her way. But between each calm cluster of families going about their dinner-time life, explosions racketed from the direction of the city center.

Bissau was turbulent. It was a city at war. Which was odd. As she understood the political structure, it was the military and the politicians who were constantly struggling for control of the drug trade. And no one else cared. For some reason, this time the entire city had erupted into violence.

It reminded her of the World Trade Organization riots she'd ridden out during the 1999 Battle of Seattle. America had managed to set a new low for international standards of supposedly peaceful protest. To quell the "peaceful" rioting and looting had required the activation of two units of the National Guard and the entire police force. Massive vandalism, tear gas, stun grenades, rubber bullets, and over five hundred arrests. Seattle had exported their new brand of peaceful-protest-gone-violent to every subsequent meeting of the WTO, the G-8, or anyone else trying to improve international relations. This had the same feel. The place had simply gone nuts.

Out here on the periphery, near the airport but not too near, the houses had mostly emptied. Everyone had either run to join the fray at either end of the main road, or run to the countryside to get out of it.

She slouched against a wall along the avenue between the airport and city center, the only four-lane road in the whole country. She heard it called the *Fera di Bandim*. She thought that *Fera* translated as "Beast" in Portuguese, but that didn't make much sense. *Bandim* was the central market, the anchor for the center of the city. Beast in the Market. Nope. Probably meant "road" in the local Kriol language, "road to market" worked. Or maybe it meant "market." Market in Bandim? She preferred her translation. A street-corner sign, rusted and tipped badly, declared it as, Avenida Combatentes de Liberdade da Pátria. Avenue of the Patriotic Combatants of the Liberation? Avenue of the fighters to liberate some guy named Pátria?

She was losing it. She knew from training and real-world experiences that her exhaustion was going to make her useless, beginning sometime within the next twenty-four hours. So, she set that as her timer and felt better for the focus. They had to get out within twenty-four hours or they were going to die here, and that wasn't on her list of things to do in Guinea-Bissau.

Beat was tempted to try the walk into town to see what was happening, perhaps she could make an international call.

"Hello. Pentagon please. Could you please send a battalion to clean this place up?" Not likely. On an open line, sure to be monitored if it even worked, she'd be dead before she hung up the phone. Stupid idea. After just forty-two hours of being awake, she already wasn't thinking straight.

Here on the "Beast" the traffic remained light. In an hour she counted seven more tacticals, though three may have been repeats roaring from town to airport and back. That she wasn't sure was another bad clue to her state of mind. She'd been awake too long already, twenty-four more might be a bad stretch, but she couldn't think of how to rescue them sooner. Actually, she couldn't think of how to rescue them at all, that's what she was really out here looking for, wasn't it? Though she couldn't tell the ambassador that, he wouldn't make it if she told him that.

Three more tanks rolled through and one of the country's six MiG-21MF fighter jets actually roared by close overhead in a display of… she had no idea what. No one had thought that any of the six were still flying.

The MiG hadn't had any bombs tucked under its wings, but it did have a very effective built-in 23mm cannon, if it was working and they had rounds. What was certain was that someone still controlled the tiny Guinea-Bissau air force and was making a statement. A statement which told her that even if she managed to sneak back to the airport, steal the embassy plane and figure out how to fly it, they'd be gunned out of the sky.

That was it.

Right there.

Beat felt as if she'd been electro-shocked awake.

They knew that there were Americans still alive on their soil. No one in the outside world would know, but someone in Guinea-Bissau did. Someone who'd counted bodies at the garage compared with the number they had called in to the custom's office before they landed.

And the Bissau-Guineans, at least whoever presently controlled their air force, didn't want them leaving. She, Ambassador Green, and Charlotte were now being hunted.

No one else in the country had access to airplanes, the airport had been empty except for the daily passenger jet out of Dakar, and even it wouldn't come in while a coup was in progress. Only the Americans, unable to fit their schedule to the one daily commercial flight, had brought their own craft. The MiG clearly said, "We will kill you if we find you."

Time to get back to work.

Beatrice found that sandals were commonly available, so she let herself drift several blocks before stealing any. That way the theft wouldn't localize their whereabouts for any militia or angry locals that came prowling. By some miracle, they'd gotten away from the airport clean, and she didn't want to risk that little sliver of security.

Food and water didn't prove hard either. Everyone was out and about with the city at war.

She went back to their hideaway by a long, circuitous route, dragging the tail of her skirt the last few hundred feet to erase her footprints.

The hut was so silent when she returned that she feared they'd actually been stupid enough to leave, or worse, been captured. She stood motionless. Staging a one-woman rescue across the landscape of Bissau wasn't her idea of a movie that had any chance of a happy ending. Rambo she wasn't.

She hadn't seen any footprints outside, but in the soft moonlight, she might have missed them.

Then she heard it.

The ambassador and his assistant were trying to be quiet. They clearly hadn't heard her return as they moaned softly together.

Beatrice moved back outside the hut and sat in the dirt, resting her back against the doorframe. It was in moonshadow, she would be close enough to invisible resting here. She could afford to wait a little while.

Sometimes people in fear for their lives needed a little privacy.

Chapter 15

B*eat really didn't need* any more alone time.

Six months she'd been traveling in Africa and, she really hated to admit it, she missed Frank. She'd decided after her parents had been such total pains about Frank, that she didn't need any family. They'd hounded her so badly about "that boy not being good enough" that she'd cut them off. Had even taken to screening her calls with the answering machine. Finally, she'd decided that no one, including Frank, would have that hold over her and she wouldn't let herself need anybody at all.

But, she hated to admit it, she'd missed him.

She'd returned from the Africa security assignment to Brooklyn both exhausted and turbo-charged. She'd showered in every barracks, hotel, and Secret Service office that had one, from Johannesburg to Cairo to Ramstein to JFK airport, trying to wash off the last six months.

She'd missed the premieres of *Field of Dreams* and *Dead Poet Society*. And she'd wager that without her guidance, or "hounding his ass" as he called it, Frank had probably gone to see nothing except *Batman* and the unpredicted hit *Bill and Ted's Excellent Adventure*. She'd been stuck with that on the commercial flight from Germany and could have shot herself. She'd fix his movie habits straight off.

After spending six months overseas, she thought maybe they could get together. At least for movies. There was no real question in her mind that Frank was the kind of man who would wait for her, simply because he said he would. He was just that much a man of his word.

The rest of it, well, she'd have to wait and see. Some great no-strings sex, that she'd definitely be up for. He'd be up for that. Wouldn't he? She certainly wasn't going to have with-strings sex, so it had better be good enough.

When she'd left, he hadn't laid any guilt trip on her about staying single or anything, but there hadn't been even one man on the road who'd measured up to the Frank Adams' standard. More than once she'd cursed the damn street punk for ruining her for casual sex with other men. Whoever she hooked up with, they had a whole new level of fine they'd have to rate. And none had.

After her third shower, a meal, and sixteen hours of sleep, just to prove she didn't need him that badly, she dialed his phone.

She had to get the Chinese grocer three times before she checked the number. She dialed it a fourth time to be sure.

Where the hell was he?

It might be six a.m. Friday morning here, but her body was still on Africa time and she'd been up for hours. Thought she was being nice by not calling him when she'd woken up at two a.m.

Well, she was supposed to have the next five days off, but it was clearly high time to head into the office. Someone would know where he'd gone.

# # #

Frank sat in the Secret Service liaison office at Fort Sam Houston. The U.S. Southern Command in San Antonio, Texas had given them one tiny room for the four of them to cram into.

He looked at his watch. Beat'd be home by now, probably still sleeping off the flight. Back from six months of silence in Africa.

He'd kept a track on her schedule, but had decided it would be better if that remained very quiet. She'd made it damn clear before she left, and by her utter lack of communication while gone, that the next move was up to her.

Focus, he ordered himself for about the four-thousandth time in the last forty-eight hours. Knowing she was on her way home, his focus had seriously sucked. Not enough for others on the Fort Sam team to comment on it, but pretty bad.

She'd missed some interesting times.

Earlier in June the Ayatollah Khomeini had died and the next day halfway around the globe had been the Tiananmen Square massacre. Two days later, back in Iran, the Ayatollah's body had almost been dumped to the ground during a hastily aborted funeral as thousands of grief-ridden mourners had tried to snag a piece of his death shroud to remember him by.

Emergency Secret Service teams had been formed to assess dangers to both U.S. diplomatic security in China and possible terrorism threats from an Islamic right wing seeking opportunities among an entire people gone mad with grief.

Frank got pulled into active service two months ago. He'd gotten his orders about two hours after he graduated training and been declared an agent. He'd made it through as head of his class, a distinction he shared with Agent Beatrice Ann Belfour. He closed his eyes for a moment, ignoring the pain that had grown as she hadn't called throughout that day. He'd known she was at the Nairobi Embassy all that week. It would have been so easy for her to find out how he was doing. Easy to have called or sent a god damn telegram. Would faxing an inter-office memo saying, "Congratulations!" have frickin' killed the woman? Apparently.

She hadn't done any of it, and that had been a bitter pill.

Focus.

He looked at the cork board he and the four other agents had been covering with information over the last two months. His first assignment had landed him on a Panama diplomatic security planning team in San Antonio. As if the back-to-back messes in Iran and China weren't enough, bloody Noriega had to add this drug-gang-boss shit on. The world was really cracking at the seams this year.

Manuel Noriega had run completely out of control. Originally nurtured to power by American support, things started to go bad in the 1970s. By 1986 it became clear that it was bad, and President Reagan had tried to force him to step down. By 1988, the Pentagon was pushing for an invasion but Reagan had refused. Presidential-hopeful Bush had ties to Noriega from his years as Director of the CIA and heading the Task Force on Drugs, and President Reagan hadn't wanted to damage his Vice-President's chances of election, so he'd held off.

It looked as if it would finally fall to President Bush to deal with his former colleague. It now appeared that Bush had carefully ignored numerous reports regarding Noriega's activities in money-laundering and drug-trafficking.

Noriega had just lost an election and then declared the results invalid. Two thousand U.S. troops had been sent in to secure American interests in the Canal Zone. And Frank's team was building scenarios on how to protect and, if necessary, cleanly extract American diplomatic personnel if it all went to hell.

The phone on the table rang and Frank answered it for something to do, because he sure hadn't been following the latest conversation on the on-going Operations Sand Flea and Purple Storm. The idea was to stage numerous military exercises in Panama that showed U.S. might, to prove "Freedom of Movement" rights throughout the Canal Zone and into surrounding countryside, as well as to utterly overwhelm and confuse Panamanian observers with the sheer volume of the exercises.

Nine different military operations, most grouped under Operation Prayer Book, formed a dazzling confusion that kept the Secret Service almost as bewildered as the Panamanians about what the American military was up to. Like an old razzle-dazzle move in a street fight. "Don't look over here, because if you do, we gone kick your sorry ass from over there."

"Adams here."

"What the hell are you doing in Texas?" Beatrice Ann Belfour sounded pissed.

And he was so damn glad to hear her voice, that his knees folded right out from under him, and he dropped into a chair. The other three guys startled and turned to see what was up. What was up was a huge grin that he couldn't stop from spreading across his face.

"Workin' is what I'm doin'."

"But in Texas?"

He loved that she was pissed that he wasn't in Brooklyn. It felt so damn good, he could really get to enjoy this. Did she even realize how upset she sounded? Man, this was the kind of ego stroke he'd been needing and needing bad.

"You missed some good movies."

She growled, actually growled at the change of topic. It also clearly told him what she'd expected him to go see. So, he didn't mention *Cyborg* with his man Van Damme kickin' ass.

"*Indiana Jones III* came out, funny as hell. Had Sean Connery as his dad, I know you're all hot for him." One of the guys in the room laughed loud enough that Frank knew the phone had picked it up and shot it straight to Beat's earpiece. Beat would know he was sitting in a room full of guys while teasing her. That should make her crazy. And worse, it really had been her kind of movie. He'd sort of gone to it so it would feel like they were connected. All it had gone and done was make him sad.

"The new *Star Trek* sort of sucked. All about Spock's brother or some kinda crap." She had a weak spot for Nimoy, too. She'd gotten him hooked on the series so he'd have gone to that one on his own anyway.

He could feel her fuming all the way down the phone line.

"Texas?" With a single snapped word, she refocused the conversation where she wanted it.

"It be where de action at, man." Again, the other agents were eyeing him strangely. They were used to his cleaned-up NYU use of language. To tease Beat, he'd slid right down into Morningside Heights street.

"What kind of action?"

"You cleared for this?" God, this was just way too much fun.

"I damn well will be." And she hung up on him.

He couldn't suppress his smile. He wasn't sure what her response would be, but he couldn't wait to find out.

Chapter 16

Frank: Now

Frank ground his teeth as the President's Southeast Asia trade meeting ran for an extra half hour. It was all he could do to retain his position at the end of the Woodrow Wilson Reading Room, the center of the Dag Hammarskjöld Library.

Down the left wall, a long line of built-in card catalogs filled the entire long wall. And the U.N. people were using them. He wasn't sure the last time he'd seen a card catalog in use. Of course, this catalog was everything from the League of Nations, which predated the U.N. A lot of what existed in this catalog were still the foundations of international law. His head hurt just thinking of the automation nightmare to catch that up.

The room was twenty-plus feet wide and about eighty long. Several low bookcases against the right-hand glass wall partially blocked his view, so he kept a very careful eye on who went to those. Frank had checked the glass and the view of the central fountain. The glass was thick enough to stop low-caliber fire. A double-tap with a big sniper rifle like a Barrett would get through and a Steyr probably wouldn't even deflect. That Steyr had designed a hand-carried rifle that could punch holes in an armored personnel carrier creeped him out.

What would it do to the "Beast" if targeted while the President was inside. It might resist it. He ran some foot-pound force comparisons in his head, Steyr vs. armor. They might be okay. The "Beast" was a tough car. But maybe not.

Deep breath. Focus.

Lesson number eight-ninety-three, worry only about what you can control. But so damn much was out of his control. Any of a half-dozen apartment buildings that he could see out the window could have a shooter on the balcony. There were a pair of Secret Service counter-snipers tasked with watching for that, but that was a whole lotta apartments to cover. And if the shooter was standing back in the shadows of an open window…

His mood had gotten way too dark.

The G-B ambassador had at least called back promptly on the hour and made it thoroughly clear, by how much he'd said without saying anything at all, that he couldn't reach anyone in his government.

The President already had U.S. armed forces moving some heavy assets down onto the Cape Verde Islands which lay just five hundred miles offshore to the northwest. The Air Force was planning to put the assets in place after dark fell there, with hopes they could be done and gone before daybreak.

There was a Carrier Strike Group within six hundred miles of Guinea-Bissau that was already shifting position. They could halve that distance in the next eight hours which would shift possible operation scenarios. The President had made it clear that he'd be moving them anyway because of the coup, but that was his careful political side talking. The comforting hand he'd rested on Frank's forearm told him that was definitely not the only reason he was moving so fast.

And Frank had no proof Agent Belfour was dead.

He needed to remember that.

The last report, between dinner and this meeting, had placed two C-135 Stratotankers, used for mid-air refueling, ready on the runway at Cape Verde. A trio of C-17 transports were also enroute from Ramstein Air Force Base in Germany with fully manned APCs in their cargo bays, just in case they found a use for Armored Personnel Carriers during the rescue. Also, one more transport with a bellyful of 75th Regiment U.S. Ranger paratroopers armed for some serious trouble, in case they needed to jump in and take the airport by force. But all that was a level of international involvement that no one on either side wanted to get into.

Except him. Right now it was a good thing he wasn't the one holding the go button.

He scanned the room again. They were in the peaceful center of the U.N.'s library. The ceiling rose in gentle, wood-sheathed waves rising from the card catalog to the outer window, which washed the room with soft northern light. At a small table near the west end of the room, President Matthews sat casually with the ambassadors of Laos and Cambodia. Also at the table were the Vietnamese ambassador and one of their Deputy Prime Ministers.

And there was a woman who was the cause of all Frank's pain.

It had started as a trade meeting, and the woman had been seated quietly between the Laos and Cambodia ambassadors. But then she'd started talking.

And the President had listened, started drawing her out, much to the consternation of the men who had thought it was their meeting.

Frank could see why she'd so grabbed the President's attention. She reminded Frank of Carole Bouquet, the Bond girl from *For Your Eyes Only*. He'd been thirteen and madly in lust with her enough to slide into the theater an extra couple times. All long dark hair, that actually billowed, light eyes, and a serious body. The best part was that she didn't hang around going, "Oh James," with a sigh. She bought a crossbow and kicked ass.

This woman looked like that, but with almond-shaped eyes and the dusky skin of a Vietnamese Eurasian. France and Vietnam twisted together into one fine-looking woman. Fine enough to turn even the President's head which was saying something. Since his own wife had died in that helicopter crash during his first year in office, he hadn't looked at a single woman. Well, except his childhood friend Emily Beale, who'd already fallen for Major Mark Henderson, even if it took her a bit to figure it out.

As the trade meeting stretched long past any reasonable ending time, she took over the conversation, gently at first, so smoothly Frank thought she'd make a good agent. There was no ripple as she took full control. Watching her political savvy, Frank moved past irritation and began to wonder more about who she really was.

"Hank," he triggered his mike and whispered into it. "I know we cleared this Kim-Ly Beauchamp. What have you got on her?"

"Chief of Unit, Southeast Asia for the World Heritage Center of UNESCO. As far as I can tell, that's a pretty serious role."

He clicked his mike once to acknowledge receipt.

"We've got scenarios for the President when he'd done."

Another click and a deep-rooted effort not to scream with impatience.

The lady wasn't making her points with her beauty, she was making it with her brains. He could hear bits and pieces about at-risk heritage sites and how their protection should be an essential requirement before the settling of any trade agreement, because they needed large levers to enforce protection of fragile environments.

Frank could get to like her, she had the Laotian and Cambodian ambassadors squirming about something, though he couldn't quite tell what. Seventeen billion dollars of yearly trade on the table compared with a couple of old temples and she was taking it on as if it made sense. He wished her luck.

The thing was, she was having some as she talked about tourism dollars. She'd sure caught the President's ear. More than his ear, she'd caught his attention.

"Hank, read me the longer version."

It all appeared very friendly, but he wasn't paid to trust to appearances. As the woman's background sounded in his ear, thankfully read by one of the techs without Hank's twisted sense of humor, he kept his eyes and his attention on the room.

Frank and the other three bodyguards lined the west wall like statues, except for their roving eyes. They each stood a little over an arm's-length apart. It provided each of them with a maximum field of vision and range of action. Frank had to admit, these guys were acting like a cut above. He'd met Kim Jong-un, the North Korean ruler's bodyguard last Christmas. He'd been less than impressed. These three guys were either trying to show off for him, the head of the U.S. Presidential Protection Detail, or they were just that damned serious about their jobs.

Probably a bit of both.

Now he just had to wait.

# # #

As they sat in darkness on the hut's dirt floor and ate the stolen spicy peanut *fufu* with their hands, the starchy cassava sticking to their fingers, Beatrice filled in the ambassador and Charlotte on the situation. Despite the food being cold, it burned the tongue and forced them all to drink a lot of water, which was good. Beat could tell by the sharp stench of their urine, despite the hole they'd dug in the corner of the hut and reburied, that they were all badly dehydrated. She was no exception, not daring to go out in the daytime to get water.

"We're being actively hunted." Beat kept her voice soft and slightly breathy. That would make it harder to distinguish directionally. "They appear to know that we survived the attack on the airport."

"But that makes no sense, why would they hunt us?" Charlotte handed her blue pumps over to Sam Green who slid them into his burlap bag with his briefcase. The sandals fit just fine and would be far more comfortable. That should help their speed.

"Regrettably, it does."

Beatrice tried to see the ambassador's face in the darkness of the hut, but couldn't make it out.

"How? I haven't been able to make sense of it."

"Last April…"

She whispered, "softly," to him and he tried, but didn't succeed much.

"… we captured their former Chief of the Navy in a drug-running and arms-trade bust at sea. He had thirty million dollars of cocaine and two dozen MANPADS." Sam Green's whisper became more assured. They were getting back into his territory.

"MANPADS?" Charlotte hadn't heard that one yet.

"Man-Portable Air-Defense Systems. Shoulder-mounted anti-aircraft missiles. They were headed to the Colombian drug lords for shooting down the U.S.'s D.E.A. helicopters. We're close to tying him back to the acting President of Guinea-Bissau and, with time, about a third of the power elite. If we can prove that, we can perhaps convince the U.N. Coalition Forces that it's time to clean this place up."

"But that didn't work in Somalia." The U.S. had tried to do exactly that about twenty years ago and the country still wasn't working.

"But Somalia," Green pointed out, "had no functioning government at that time. G-B still does, mostly. If we can get control of that back into the voters' hands, where their constitution says it belongs, this country might stand a chance."

"And that's what's in your briefcase."

"Right," he rested a protective hand on his burlap bag. "I'm carrying a proposal to the people we were unable to connect to the drug-running, and if they agree, we'll land heavily on their side. If we can even get U.N. peacekeepers and international election monitors in the door, maybe we can start working on free elections and shifting their economy off the drug trade. Then, eventually, we can end this disaster that started the day they claimed independence in 1973. But these documents also include their names, a death sentence to these people who might be our friends, and the death of all our hopes if it falls into the wrong hands. My notes and appointments would become a kill-list of every potentially reliable politician and leader."

Maybe he wasn't quite the lost cause Beatrice had thought him to be. Terrified out of his skull, definitely, but he'd hung onto that stupid briefcase for a reason. And maybe something about making love to Charlotte in a darkened West African hut, or being hunted like a criminal, had given him a focus.

"But why would they want to kill you?"

He shrugged. His white *dashiki* just catching the light from the one window to reveal the gesture.

"Different factions. One faction sees a chance to lash out at the U.S. by killing me, not realizing the world of hurt that will land down upon them should they succeed in doing so. The more rational factions think my death would send a clear message to stay out of G-B politics, not that it would work any better. Others would perchance prefer me alive as a bargaining chip. They'd use me to save their own skins with transport to a country they can disappear in, the Congo and Senegal don't have an extradition treaty with us. Perhaps a few people think they can gain a favor from the U.S. government if they save my life, maybe the politicians and military leaders on my list, but maybe not. How can I tell them from the others until we've had a chance to meet and talk?"

Beatrice let it all process. It fit. Not all of it, but enough that she knew what was going on and what had to come next.

"Okay, this is going to get harder, starting right now. Are you two up for it?"

By their too-bright hair, she could see them turning toward one another. Sam reached out and took Charlotte's hand, then brought it to his lips.

They turned back to Beat.

"Okay, we're ready."

Beatrice moved to the door, checked both directions, listening to the silence of the streets, and moved them out. They had four, perhaps five more hours of darkness and a lot of ground to cover.

Chapter 17

Beat: 1989

Half a step before storming into the conference room at Fort Sam Houston, in San Antonio, Texas, Beat stopped herself.

Secret Service liaison office to U.S. Southern Command regarding the Panama situation.

This was Frank's first assignment, a huge feather in his cap to be assigned the project straight out of training. She'd gotten some of the history on it. The whole thing was tiny when it started, so they sent down a senior agent and three rookies, one of which was Frank. Two months in, the senior guy got offered a cherry assignment. He'd insisted that one of the rookies had it in hand, so rather than send a new lead, they'd sent the new leader a mid-level guy to help.

So what had she done?

She'd gone from six months in Africa to being assigned to the Panama mission in under seventy-two hours.

By being so angry at Frank Adams that she hadn't been thinking, was how she'd done it. Beatrice had blown through the Secret Service command hierarchy so fast that she'd bet her section commander had shipped her out just to be rid of her demands to be assigned to the Panama project.

Panama? What the heck was up with that?

She'd landed from Africa Wednesday night, slept most of Thursday, tracked Frank down on Friday morning, and was supposed to have the week off but instead been on the road by that night. She'd driven twenty-four of the last forty-eight hours, crashing into a Motel 6 in Chattanooga, Tennessee for fourteen hours in the middle of it. Now it was Monday morning, July third at eight a.m. She was in San Antonio, Texas and through the Fort Sam security.

And Panama?

If she went storming into the Secret Service liaison office, Frank would just laugh his head off and she'd be forced to kill him. And she sure didn't like the idea of being one of the peons like he was, but she didn't want to start a battle for control either. Her section commander had made it clear that some new agent was shaping up well and they were going to let him run with it and see how he did. He'd told her that they were only letting her jump on because she'd done so well in Africa, but it wasn't her team.

So, one, she didn't want to tromp on his toes.

Two, the fact that she'd showed up at all... well, he'd know he'd won. She hadn't thought of that. She'd just been so damn angry she hadn't been thinking right up to this moment. He'd made her angrier than the day he'd tried to carjack her new car. And she was angry now for his not being where she'd left him.

That in itself was pretty damn stupid. Of course he'd take a great opportunity like this one.

She didn't like these feelings one bit for a whole lot of reasons.

She turned and walked back to the white porcelain water fountain hanging from a gray tile wall between the bathrooms. She wasn't thirsty, though her throat was dry. She just needed a moment to think.

Beat knew that if she were rational, she'd go and climb back into her car and head right back to Brooklyn, to beg for a new assignment.

No strings. No ties. Her parents had always been trying to tie her in knots to fit their plans for her. It had sure worked on her sister. Hannah had a degree in literature, a pediatrician husband she'd met at Vassar and helped support through Columbia, two cute kids, and she was barely twenty five. They'd just bought their first place barely ten blocks from her parents' place, serious parent heaven. Hannah's life was all neat and set. And it probably was, her husband was a great guy. Good for her.

Not for Beat.

Over the last six months she'd finally decided that she liked her new nickname, even if Frank Adams had been the one to give it to her. Beat was a tougher, stronger woman than Beatrice Ann. Beat wouldn't be shying away from facing Frank Adams. She'd just sweep into that conference room and take over.

She turned, made sure her vest hung straight and headed for the office door. Just as she hit the door she realized that, without thinking, she was wearing the exact clothes she'd been wearing when she first met him.

Well, he better not get all smug, or he'd be going down.

Going down hard.

# # #

Frank heard the door slam open, rocketing into Malcolm's desk with a sharp thwack. He didn't even bother to turn, he knew exactly who stood now in the doorway behind him.

The other three guys, so used to the banging door they didn't jump, did turn to look. Frank could see by their total shift of concentration just how much they appreciated the vision standing there.

He turned his chair slowly from where he'd been studying the latest information regarding the thirty-five thousand Americans living and working in the Canal Zone.

Beatrice Ann Belfour looked incredible. The first time he'd seen her in these clothes, it had been in the darkness of a New York City hot-summer night. Now she was lit by the Texas sunlight streaming in through the window. The damn woman shimmered.

He made a point of inspecting her exactly as he had so long ago in the underground garage at the Secret Service building. Her red sneakers had been replaced by blood-red cowboy boots, but the jeans were still tight, the lemon-yellow blouse brought her glowing skin to life, and the leather vest that he now knew was almost as soft as her skin had just enough bulge to show that she was packing her revolver in its normal shoulder holster. Her hair was about six inches longer, she hadn't cut it since they'd met, and it now fell in a glorious thick wave well past her shoulder.

And those dark eyes were boring holes right into him.

"Hey, Beat." He made it sound as casual as he could. It took effort 'cause he was so damn glad to see her.

"Hey, Adams." She didn't move, just stood there letting him drink his fill of her.

He'd never get enough. He knew he'd missed her, but had no idea how much until she stood there in front of him.

Gone, Adams. You're twenty-one and you're completely and totally gone. That wasn't supposed to happen until he'd played the field much wider and longer. It was something he'd never expected. Find a woman someday, sure. A main squeeze. But in the six months she'd been gone, he hadn't even noticed another woman. Oh, he'd had offers, but there was not a one for him other than Beat Belfour.

Then she glanced over his head at the other three guys, "So, who's in charge here?"

Frank let the silence stretch a bit before drawling out an answer.

"It's gonna really suck for you…"

Her eyes came back to his. She glared at him with that splendid mix of arrogance and pride, of a woman who knew she was just that damn good. Then a bit of smile that she did her best to hide with a scowl.

"You."

"Me."

# # #

Frank had sort of forgotten how good she was. By lunchtime he had Beat up to speed with what it had taken his team three months to gather together, by mid-afternoon she was adding ideas to his scenario planning. And he was loving it. It was like there was some kinda hyperactive feedback loop between them and the ideas just circulated back and forth between them. The other guys had gone, but he'd stuck around to show her what they knew and they'd taken off from there.

"So they're mobilizing everything?"

"Rangers, Delta, Air Force, Special Forces choppers, everything. All running as exercises now, but everyone knows they're gearing up for a big hit. We're doing a razzle-dazzle down there, moving troops in and out so fast that no Panamanians can count 'em and make a counter-plan."

"Choppers, huh?"

Frank glanced down at the paperwork. "Some outfit called the 160th Special Operations Group. What are you thinking?"

Beat just smiled at him. He could see that something had just clicked in her brain and she wasn't going to share it yet. So, he looked for a change of topic.

"It's July 3rd, you know."

"Yeah," she said it like it was nothing important and that pissed him off some.

The other agents had left after lunch. They had families in the area. Only he and Beat had stayed. The heat in the office had gone up several degrees since lunch even though the sun had moved around the other side of the building. It forced Frank to loosen his collar. The four white walls covered with maps pressed in around the four desks and table, all crammed into a space that had probably been one man's office prior to the Secret Service's arrival. Gearing up for a potential invasion of Panama had made space a premium at Fort Sam.

"What I'm thinking… " she drew out the words in a way that definitely made him think some very nice things.

God, she was muddling his brain. All he knew was that he wanted to get his hands on Beatrice Ann Belfour and he didn't care how, as long as it was soon.

It was a trap. Had to be.

"I'm thinking that I saw a place on the drive in that's still running *Ghostbusters II*. Want to go?"

"You hate sequels."

"You love Sigourney Weaver."

Yep. A complete and total trap.

Chapter 18

Frank: Now

W*hat do we know* about her?"

"Who?" Frank knew exactly who the President was talking about, but he wasn't going to let him off that easy. They were effectively alone, walking through the underground corridor that connected the Dag Hammarskjöld Library with the Secretariat Tower. Two agents cleared the corridor ahead and two followed behind.

"Don't give me a hard time here, Frank."

"Or what, sir?"

"Or I'll name Beat the head of my detail when she gets back and put you somewhere you can be of use like an Alaskan sewage treatment plant."

Damn he liked working for this man. He took a joke and built in a ray of hope and confidence that Frank sure wasn't feeling.

"Kim-Ly Geneviève Beauchamp, mixed French and Vietnamese descent, French side came to Vietnam in the 1930s. Traditional plantation owners. Had to leave to avoid the War and the Reeducation Camps, but the ties were too deep and they came back almost right away. She was born there. Educated John Hopkins and Cambridge, the one in England."

"A Cambrian?"

"Cambrian, sir?"

"If it weren't a proper noun it would be a good Scrabble word, with the C, M, and B it's worth thirteen points and is eight letters long, a good length. If you can find just one letter to play off, you can score an extra fifty point Bingo for clearing your tray. Cambrian is from an old story at Oxford. We always said Cambridge was found by some Oxfordians who couldn't cut it. So they were banished to the fens, the marshes, and founded a silly little school named Cambridge. Cambrian is an ancient geologic age, out of date, slow. Worse, she's probably a Cavendisher, one of the all-women colleges at the University."

Frank had no idea what he was talking about, but he seemed pretty pleased by it all. Frank turned back to his report. "Straight to UNESCO, now Chief of Unit for World Heritage of Southeast Asia. Very determined lady. Cavendisher by the way is a also proper noun, so you don't get to use that one either."

President Matthews nodded his head and kept his silence as they continued down the corridor. At the stairs they went down one flight to get to the United States Security Center.

The President was thinking some pretty serious thoughts when he didn't even smile at a Scrabble-based tease.

Frank knew that silence. Knew it from deep inside when he'd waited in Texas wondering when he'd get to see Beatrice Belfour again.

He offered the President the next layer.

"Thirty-two years old, married once, didn't stick. Broke off with last boyfriend two weeks after being named Chief of Unit last year. Word is he didn't like that her career was dusting his, a German named Klaus of all things."

That actually got the President to stop right before they went through the outer security door. That caused the other agents up and down the hall some consternation, but Frank flickered an "all okay" sign and just waited.

Nothing.

President Matthews' face was normally intensely expressive, man couldn't play poker to save his life as his friend Mark Henderson kept proving to him time and again. And right now it was very carefully showing nothing.

Frank whistled quietly to himself. How long had the President been in conference with her? An hour, a little more.

He thought back to the day he'd met Beat. Once around the nose of her BMW, he could easily have run. Cops might have laid chase, but he'd have a pretty good chance of making it clean. She probably had expected him to. But something about her made it so that he got in the car. He'd stood there for three heartbeats, then trusted her with his life. It had been that fast. At least for him. He'd seen that lady with the dark, dark eyes and just had to know more.

"I bet, Mr. President, that she'd be glad of a chance to do a lecture series at George Washington University or something like that."

"Are you trying to matchmake me, Frank?"

"No sir, Mr. President. Just thinking out loud, sir."

They walked through the outer door of the basement security offices together, Frank flashed a hand signal clearing the other agents in the hall to close the distance from either end of the hall and to take up station on the door.

While the outer and inner door bolts were shifting with their sharp metallic buzzes, the President spoke without looking up at him.

"So, maybe I'll keep you around after all. Now let's go see about getting Agent Belfour in from whatever limb she's stuck out on."

Frank followed him in with the first feeling of hope he'd had all day.

"By the way, Frank, 'cavendish' is a sweet tobacco cake. So I can use it. Seventeen points."

# # #

"The problem we have, Mr. President, is that we have no way to contact any assets on the ground, or even determine if they're still alive to do so." Chairman of the Joint Chiefs of Staff Brett Rogers stared at them out of their screen which linked to the White House Situation Room.

So much for hope. Frank resisted the urge to lay his head down on the table.

Once again, the President sat at the head of the table. Frank and Hank sat to either side. Frank had sat, 'cause otherwise he'd pace and that wouldn't help anything.

In the hour since they'd been gone to the U.N. meeting with Southeast Asia, the staff in the room had been sharply upgraded. The left-hand seats along the wall were now filled with Army, Navy, Air Force, and Special Forces reps, all officer ranks. They each had direct links to their superiors sitting to either side of General Rogers in the Situation Room as well as to whatever other points of contact they needed.

The screens which had held a few photos of the plane, garage, and burning liaison office in Guinea-Bissau were now filled with images of the center of downtown Bissau. Dozens of buildings were on fire. Two dozen tanks were scattered about the town like dropped toys, except several of them were burning as well.

"Intramural. The Army is fighting itself," the President observed.

"That and probably worse. Only the core of the town has ever had cell phone service, but Guinetel pulled the plug on that, or someone pulled it for them, about six hours ago. Phones aren't exactly common either, especially not outside the core. There aren't more than a couple dozen Internet lines for public use in the whole city, fastest thing they've got wouldn't run my four-year-old grandkid's MathWiz game. But they pulled the plug on those too. So not even Twitter to give us ground intel as there would be in any other disaster of a nation. The only people with satellite phones are the drug lords, and they're all lying low or engaged in the battle. We've kicked a Global Hawk drone into the air and it should be on site shortly. We're hoping we can grab some radio chatter. The Raptor we sent earlier was an imaging bird, doesn't have the heavy intel-gathering package."

It was all still a jumble.

Frank looked about the room and tried to spot why. Everyone was doing their thing. The screens to either side of the Chairman of the Joint Chiefs were alive with data. But it didn't feel right.

He'd ridden out enough of these with the President now to know that when they were on the track of a solution, even if it wasn't there yet, you could taste the crackle of it in the air.

This air tasted of nothing but air conditioning and worry.

He looked at the satellite photo of Bissau taken on the last pass before darkness had fallen.

It was midnight there now.

It was time to be on the move.

But each time she moved, Beat would become harder to find. Clearly, going back to the airport hadn't been her first choice. Couldn't blame her since she'd already lost two people there. By now Beat would know that downtown wasn't worth risking either. Not even on the chance of finding a working cell tower.

"Cell phones."

"What?" The buzz of conversation dropped. The others had been talking about something else. Mapping patterns of unexpected thermal movement. Like that would work in a city of a couple hundred thousand people with a coup going on.

"They've shut off the cell towers, Frank." General Rogers and he had become friends over their last few years serving together at the White House.

"Right," Frank could see the idea forming in his head. "But maybe Agent Belfour hasn't shut off her own phone. Do the Raptor or Global Hawk have cell phone scanners? Can we piggyback it onto a radio and talk to them?"

One of the techs on the left-side of the U.N. security office must have put up a request to join the conference. The Marine Corps intelligence officer who was running the conference popped an image of the tech's face into the lower corner of the main screen. Navy Lieutenant, cute Asian woman, sitting third down the left-wall row.

"Sir, the Global Hawk drone as rigged can only receive calls for monitoring purposes. But the Raptor bird already on site for imaging had been previously tasked for alert broadcast to all cell phones in an area. That hardware is still aboard. It will take some time to set up, but we should be able to transmit with one bird and receive with the other."

"Get it built. You've got twenty minutes until everything is on site."

Twenty minutes. Frank closed his eyes and tried to do one of those telepathy things like in the movies. He'd be the first one ever to successfully send a telepathic message and save a life.

"Stay low, be careful," he thought as loudly as he could.

# # #

"Why can't we just steal the plane?" Ambassador Green whispered from close beside Beat. At least he'd learned to keep his voice down.

They squatted close beside the wreckage of the garage. Still no one had come to clean it up. The flesh of the pieces of the two embassy personnel killed in the explosion had started to go putrid in the tropical heat. There was a slight land breeze headed out to sea, so she moved them to the upwind, east side of the garage to cut the smell.

When Charlotte and Sam had asked what that stench was, she hadn't answered. Thankfully they already knew to never ask her something a second time. They'd learned that she always heard them and when she didn't respond it was because they didn't want to know. Not the screaming of a burn victim, nor the wailing of half the family as they were told the other half was now dead.

"Can you fly a plane?"

"Always meant to learn, but no. Can't you?"

Like she was some sort of miracle girl. Actually, she'd be willing to try if it weren't for the two tacticals parked at the other end of the main terminal. Their crews might be asleep and/or drunk, but they'd snap to the moment she tried cranking over the plane's engines. Two turret-mounted machine guns would make a real mess of the plane and any passengers long before they reached takeoff speed.

No, she had a different plan.

"Wait here." While she'd been out prowling earlier, she'd traded her blue *pagne* and skirt for a dark *dashiki* and loose pants that would allow her move well.

She slid up to the bottom of the plane's fold-down steps and waited. She'd found a cooking knife during her prowl and held it hidden in her hand, the blade held flat against her wrist. While it was no K-bar survival blade, it would be quieter than her Sig Sauer. Though she made sure that too was close to hand.

The pilot's large blood stain at the base of the steps had dried, not even the flies could find anything more there. She spotted his body shoved under one of the wings.

The lights were out over the whole airport, only the moonlight had revealed the tacticals. The steps were still hanging down and the inside of the plane was pitch dark. The third of the four steps creaked and the plane rocked ever so slightly on its shocks as she climbed aboard. Up the narrow aisle between the facing pairs of armchairs with the little tables between them to either side. Not even the smell of stale peanuts remained.

The cockpit was quiet and the moonlight through the windshield let her see enough to find the switch for the panel lights.

She turned them on with a flick and saw that she was screwed.

The pilot must have been trying to radio for help after the garage blew up, before being dragged from the plane. Whoever took him had shot the radios. Five neat shots right through the faces of each radio and transponder. No calling for help from here. She shut off the panel lights.

She knew the King Air had an ELT in the tail, but she wasn't exactly sure where. Emergency Locator Transmitters triggered for crashes. They must have manual switches. If not, she would beat it with a length of steel pipe until it decided to cry for help.

It would be a messy call, ELTs were designed to scream long and loud on common radio frequencies, but at least it would tell someone to come looking for them.

She was halfway back through the plane when an alarm burst out in the cabin.

Not an alarm!

Her cell phone.

It rang again so loudly in the plane she almost wanted to cover her ears. It vibrated harshly against her rib cage, under the *dashiki* in the pocket of the shirt she'd kept on beneath her native clothes.

She bent over to dig for it under the layers of cloth.

As she did so, a roar and flash slapped at her, knocking her sideways into a seat with the sheer force of the concussion.

Another burst and she saw the origin.

Bending over had saved her life.

Someone had been asleep in the back of the plane, probably after raiding the tiny galley. Someone with a rifle.

Woken by the cell phone, he'd fired wildly at her inside the plane. Her ears still rang, the only thing she could hear, though the cell phone buzzed once more against her rib cage.

Blinded by his own rifle fire, the man stumbled forward down the aisle.

Go just one more step, she coaxed him forward.

He fired at the cockpit again, shattering the windshield. The spent cartridge casing ejected right past her head, fast, and pinged off one of the windows. Had to be a Czech VZ with that kind of ejection. Amazing that the thing still worked, it should be in a museum.

In the light of the muzzle flash, he saw his mistake. She was lying mostly in one of the seats, now right beside him.

As he turned, she struck.

She'd kept the blade despite the shock and with a single stroke she dragged it across his jugular vein and throat.

Hot blood splashed her face and arm. She was moving before he hit the floor. He was still trying to gasp his final breath when she dove out the door and hit the tarmac. With a fast roll she regained her feet and sprinted back to the protection of the garage.

Sweeping up Sam and Charlotte, she raced into the night.

Behind them the tacticals opened up on the plane even as their drivers raced the Toyotas to redline, sprinting down the field.

There was a low cough, like the world catching its breath, and Beat dragged her two charges to the ground.

The plane blew with a deafening roar that lit the night sky like a torch a dozen stories high.

One of the tacticals, its driver still too drunk or hung over or asleep to compensate, twisted the wheels on his truck sharply while traveling too fast. The vehicle rolled into the burning airplane taking its driver and gun crew with it.

Their screams didn't last long.

While the other tactical was distracted by the mayhem, the three of them slipped further into the night.

# # #

"What the hell happened?" Frank's roar filled the room. It wasn't his place, but he couldn't help himself. One moment they'd had a clear ring tone on Beat's cell phone and the next it looked like the airport had blown up.

"Someone get me a clear shot of the airport," General Brett Rogers snarled out. Frank had never heard that tone from the Chairman of the Joint Chiefs before and decided he'd better shut up.

A tech sent the command to some obscure bunker, probably in Utah, and the remote pilot sent his command over satellite to turn the Raptor's camera. Moments later it centered on the flame. One tactical had rolled in and also burned, they could see the bright sparkles of the ammunition firing off in the intense heat at the heart of the fire.

The other truck was backing off slowly, being beaten away by the heat.

"Someone roll back the footage."

Moments later they were staring at the long view with the airport off in the corner of the picture. It was a ghostly image of greens and blacks that came from infrared cameras for night vision. Cooking fires flared bright in some of the surrounding neighborhood. No streetlights or houselights. Power was out in the largest city in the country.

"Zoom and enhance," Rogers ordered. "C'mon people. Think ahead. Work the problem."

The resolution was lousy, but in moments the little embassy plane filled the screen, a dull green cross a couple-dozen image pixels square against the cooler black of the airport parking area.

"There!" Frank pointed. A lone figure, about ten pixels big but large enough to see how carefully they were moving, sidled up to the plane.

"That's got to be Beat. No one moves like that but a trained agent." She was alive. Frank had never been so glad to see a heat trace. Or she'd been alive three minutes ago.

The silence in the room echoed as the video spooled in real time.

The three pixels at the nose of a plane brightened.

The Navy tech whose face had remained in the corner of screen reported, "Brightness change approximately equal to control panel lights."

Before he could wonder if Beat was going for flight or radios, the brightness disappeared. She'd made it to the cockpit and either found what she'd wanted, or what she'd hoped to find wasn't there. He knew the pilot was dead. He also knew she didn't know how to fly.

"Radios. She went after the radios. They must not have been usable. That's why—"

"Here's where her phone rang," the tech cut him off.

Nothing.

"Agai—"

Before the tech could finish, a flash of light, and another. The brightness shone out all of the side windows on the side facing the Raptor's camera flying far overhead.

"Brightness change indicates gunfire. Single rounds."

One more.

Their phone call had gotten her shot. Someone asleep on the plane, and they'd woken him with a goddamn phone call. His idea had gotten her killed.

"Phone signal lost."

Then a figure dove out of the door, did a hit-roll-run combo that every aching inch of his body knew by heart. And she'd just done it out an airplane door opening five feet above hard tarmac. That had to hurt.

But Beat was alive. It was all he needed to know. She was alive. Relief flooded through him like a salve to his soul. The world just wouldn't be a worthwhile place without her in it.

The tech followed her. She swept up two other dim figures of only a few pixels each some distance from the plane and disappeared back into the city right off the edge of the Raptor's field of view.

She'd kept the ambassador and one of his assistants alive.

Damn she was good.

Chapter 19

1989: Frank

Beat wasn't the only one with tricks up her sleeve. After the *Ghostbusters II* matinee at the East San Antonio six-plex, which was only okay, though Sigourney had been damn hot, Frank got Beat into her car. But he managed to snag the keys and settle her in the passenger seat. Still exhausted from her cross-country drive, she'd obviously been feeling weak and pliable. And he wanted to keep her that way.

He took the northern route across town from Fort Sam, telling her he had a special spot for dinner. Which he did. It was Monday, July 3rd. Because most folks didn't have to work tomorrow, San Antonio was having the big city party tonight. They'd met one year ago tomorrow.

He merged into the late afternoon mayhem, got as close to Woodlawn Lake Park as he could in the thick traffic and parked it. The temp was 90s-ugly falling toward 70s-not-quite-so-ugly. It was a little cooler by the lake, but about a hundred thousand people were showing up. Here, instead of July Fourth smelling like hot dogs and sauerkraut in Manhattan, it smelled of roasted chilies and fresh salsa. Temperature, though, was about equally brutal.

The food vendors were doing an awesome business, and he and Beat snagged some fish tacos and lemonade and chose their spot by the lake. It wasn't packed solid with people yet, still an hour or so until the fireworks. The all-dayers were there with kids and float rafts and picnic baskets and blankets and sunburns and all that noise.

He and Beat just took an empty spot and sat back on the grass. The lake was a couple hundred yards across and folks were still out in those little paddlewheelers for two. The cops actually had a couple of power boats on the water ready to chase away anyone who tried to get too close to the fireworks setup.

Frank would start mellow, pick a safe topic.

They talked about Africa. Security standards. Communication. They wandered through the best summer street food in New York. As the evening light settled toward fireworks dark, he went back to her comment from the afternoon. The crowds were pretty serious now. Everyone jabbering excitedly on too much sugar and anticipation. They could have shouted the combination to the Fort Knox bullion repository and no one would have noticed.

"You said something about helicopters."

"Yeah."

Frank liked how they could pick up a conversation hours later and stay on the same page. She was so easy to be with.

"Panama City is going to be a mess."

Frank pictured the maps and reconnaissance photos that were covering their office walls. A mess was an understatement. The Panama Defense Force was everywhere. Multiple airports, not counting the one at the far end of the canal. Taking them all out while trying not to kill the thirty-five thousand Americans living there would be a good trick. Taking out radio and television stations another one. And on top of all that, bag the Pineapple himself. Dictator Manuel Noriega had an acne-pocked face, and some brilliant Army guy had dubbed him the 'Pineapple.' Did they hire people to be that stupid on purpose? Worse, the name had stuck.

"You said they're banking hard on these helicopter pilots."

"SOAG, Special Operations Aviation Group. These guys apparently kicked some serious ass in Grenada and the Persian Gulf on some piracy gig. It looks like the powers that be are having them play front and center."

"Where are they stationed?"

"Fort Campbell, Kentucky."

"Good. I have to go visit those guys."

Frank rubbed a hand across his eyes. She'd just gotten here about eight hours ago and she was already planning on leaving.

He sat up.

Would have gotten to his feet to leave if she hadn't stopped him with a hand on his shoulder.

"Not right away."

He kept his back to her, just sat there and stared at all the happy families. The ones where the women could sit still for thirty damn seconds without picking the next battle and rushing off to it. How was he supposed to survive this?

She shifted until she was kneeling in front of him.

"Hey."

She inspected his face and he managed not to look away. He watched the rapid shift of emotions. He'd been trained to see it. He could see it at the macro level where hate, anger, or fear rippled so fast that the people in a crowd didn't have time to register the sudden change, they simply felt it. He'd also learned to see it in an individual face. And he knew no face better than the one looking at him from less than a foot away.

It started coy, playful, with that wonderful hint of sex that always seemed to dance around the corners of her mouth. Then it shifted. First uncertainty, the tightness in brows, the smile sliding off the lips. The widening of the eyes and slackening of the jaw as surprise rippled through on its way to…

It had been a single year since he'd met Beatrice Belfour and signed up for training. They had beaten, chased, challenged, and strained him past anything he'd imagined possible. They made living in the projects look easy by comparison.

None of that had prepared him for the final expression hardening on her features. The narrowing of eyes, clenching of jaw, the head pulling back as if trying to retreat before the body could get the message to move away.

"No, Frank. This wasn't the goddamn deal."

He hadn't meant for it show, how much he wanted her. How much he needed her. He could feel the pain shifting to anger but couldn't stop it. Could feel his teeth ache with the pressure and the forward lean. His head shifting forward "like a goddamn pug dog," he really wished the instructor had given him a different image for that emotion.

Then it blew out of him. Beat Belfour brought cold, but Frank's anger brought heat.

"No, it's not your goddamn deal, Be-a-trice, but it is mine." He gritted his teeth to keep his voice low. Of course it was this conversation that the fat ladies on the next blanket over suddenly decided to listen to.

"I found the woman I want, but she doesn't want me. So go fly off and see the flyboys."

He struggled to his feet and dropped her car keys in front of her.

"Happy anniversary, Agent Belfour." He had to space his words around the opening salvo of fireworks bursting overhead like a howitzer. "Pleasure seeing you again."

He turned and walked away. It was the hardest damn thing he'd ever done.

# # #

Beat didn't show up at Fort Sam Houston on Tuesday. No one did except Frank. It was a national holiday, everyone else was busy celebrating or relaxing somewhere.

He received her first report Wednesday morning. She'd somehow managed to embed herself as the Secret Service liaison to the Army's immensely secretive 160th aviation group.

It was hard to credit the tactical capabilities she was reporting. These guys were as crazy as the Secret Service in their training habits. Night vision was still so new that Frank hadn't even been trained on it yet, and these guys had been flying helicopters at night for two years using that technology.

They redesigned their choppers just as thoroughly as the Secret Service redesigned Presidential planes, choppers, and cars. He'd tried to get on the 747 team, but that was a seriously huge step that not even a top-of-class rookie could hope for. Developing the next Air Force One was a cherry assignment and only cool guys with tons of experience got it. He hadn't even gotten a letter, his application had simply been returned with a small, red tick mark in the "Not accepted" box.

At first he always had the other guys process her reports.

As time passed, he started reading her reports rather than his team's summaries. She sent them to the team from stranger and stranger places. One came from D.C., though he knew she was in Miami at Hurlburt Field watching scenario practice. Then one routed through the New York office that talked about a simulation flight in Panama. It was like she'd somehow become disconnected from him and from wherever she was in world at the same time.

Sometimes he held a report and wondered if she still truly existed.

Each one he opened was fascinating, and ripped out his gut all over again. There was nothing personal in them, not a single thing. But he could still hear her voice in the writing.

As specialists in head-of-state protection, the Secret Service was getting pulled in on planning for Operation Nifty Package, pulled in by the point guard of Beatrice Ann Belfour.

Inside the overarching Operation Just Cause, intended to depose Noriega and neutralize the brutal Panama Defense Force, the combined military and secret police force, lay a smaller, trickier task.

Noriega had been convicted as a drug trafficker by a U.S. Federal Court. The U.S. government didn't want a dictator-martyr on their hands. It could destabilize a half-dozen other countries. They wanted him alive. That was Operation Nifty Package.

They tracked down his personal jet and a damn serious little gunboat. They pinpointed a dozen villas, uncovered several mistresses, and a thousand little habits. This was all fed into the overall Nifty Package plan through the conduit of Beat and Frank.

The game was escalating. He no longer had time to be pissed at her.

Hell, he didn't even have time to sleep. It was mid-December and soon, very soon, the game would be on.

Chapter 20

Beat: Now

*W*hat happened?"

Charlotte had collapsed, Green had grabbed Beat's arm, and they'd all swerved and tumbled together behind a stone wall that was probably a goat pen. It sure stank like one. Her side ached as if they'd run a hundred miles, not less than one. Her right knee was screaming, must have twisted it when she dove out of the plane. The moon had set and the world had gone pitch dark, the last fifteen minutes were more about stumbling into things than running.

About three a.m. local would be her best guess.

"What happened?" Green shook her arm and it hurt.

"They shot the radios."

"While you were in the plane?"

"Before. When they killed the pilot, they shot the radios."

"Then what was all the shooting when you were in there?"

"What, Green, is this twenty questions?"

"Yes, it's our lives too. Now what happened?"

Beat lay her head back against the stone wall, glad of the darkness. Glad that Ambassador Green couldn't see the blood sprayed all over her face. She'd tried to wipe it off her face as they ran. Even if she'd succeeded, it didn't matter, she could still feel it. Imprinted there. All that training just hadn't prepared her for the first time she'd killed a man. She'd been in the Service for, gods, two-and-a-half decades, and this had been her first one.

In the past she'd always managed to take them down, captured for questioning. She'd been with agents who'd taken down a shooter, but she'd never had to do it herself. All she wanted to do was curl up and shake for a while.

Charlotte wasn't even doing that. She was simply collapsed across their feet, too exhausted and strained to even weep. She just lay there until the time when they'd make her get up and run again.

Beat couldn't afford to do that no matter how envious she was. And Green was right, his life was on the line as much as hers.

"My phone rang."

"I thought you said there was no cell service here."

"There isn't."

"Then how."

"I'm not sure." But she had an idea. She looked up at the sky. Was someone up there watching them? Forty hours. They'd been missing for forty hours, someone had to be looking for them. Other than the Guinea-Bissau militia. She liked the idea of Frank up in the sky watching over her. Assuming he even knew. G-B wasn't exactly his area of concern, his job was the President. Still, she liked the idea that it had been him calling.

She dug for the phone, wincing at the sharp pain all along her ribs. She wasn't winded, well, not only winded. Her ribs felt as if they were cracked. She'd hit something hard.

Pulling out the phone, she scanned around to see if anyone was in sight on the streets. She couldn't see anyone or much of anything in the darkness other than the dull red light of a dying cooking fire in a hut a couple dozen yards down the road, so there was no way to tell. The smell of burning cow dung from the fire added to the goat pen in a most unpleasant way.

She and Green huddled over the phone to shield as much of the light as possible. She stroked a finger over the glass to wake up the phone. It was rough, jagged. She'd dropped enough smartphones in her day to know that was a bad sign. Though sometimes they still worked even if cracked.

The light came on and revealed a shattered screen.

She rubbed at her ribs again under the stolen *dashiki*. Her skin over the ribs was especially tender exactly in the shape of the phone.

But what had she hit? Casting her mind back, she reviewed the events of the last thirty minutes. Was that all it had been? Her mind assured her that was the case.

She'd been fine entering the plane, then the fight. Next time she'd go in with her gun drawn and cocked. And check the rear of the plane before going to the front.

There'd been the fall into the chair and hitting the table, but that had been her other side. She could feel that bruise, but it was no worse than an average training blow.

The butt of the rifle. He'd rammed it into her side even as she'd killed him. If not for the phone taking the blow, he'd probably have busted her ribs right into her lung and she'd have burned to death gasping for her own last breath right alongside him.

Almost killed by the ringing of the bell, she'd also been saved by it.

"No way to see who called. No way to call them back. Where's your phone?"

Green hesitated long enough for the answer to be clear.

"You left it on the plane because you knew the service here is so bad?"

"Not worth carrying around," his whisper was deeply chagrined. "It's so useless here. I think I successfully have made three calls in three years, and Guinetel can't link you to international, or won't. The SUVs have, had, satellite phones. That doesn't help us much now. Wish I'd tossed the phone in my briefcase this time."

"Me too." Beat started to laugh at the friendly moment, but decided against it when she felt the pull on her battered ribs.

She powered the phone off. She almost threw it away, but instead shoved it back in her pocket. It had saved her life once already. It deserved being laid to rest in some trash heap better than this place.

After considering for a few seconds, she revised the clock in her head. Their chances of making it through another day were not good. Her target of "rescued by tomorrow evening" wasn't going to cut it.

They'd have to be rescued by sunrise or they'd be goners.

# # #

"Signal lost."

Frank was going to kill the technician. They'd only just cracked into Beat's "lost my phone" automatic locator application.

"It appears she turned off her phone. Or perhaps the battery died."

"I'll kill her. I'm going to kill her if she lives through this."

The President had delayed the return flight to D.C. The situation was either going to resolve in the next three hours or not until tomorrow night. If the latter, they could fly back to D.C. while Beatrice laid low for one more day. But based on the firefight they'd just witnessed, he didn't like the chances if they had to delay through another Guinea-Bissau day. Didn't like them at all.

In the meantime, the next shift of agents had escorted the President off to meetings with the U.N. ambassadors for Senegal, The Gambia, and Guinea, the three bordering nations. The President had insisted that Frank stay as long as it took to recover Agent Belfour and her charges. Frank had managed not to kiss the man in thanks.

Word was, France and the Secretary-General were in on the meeting. Coups were rarely an improvement on regional stability. And while the French embassy hadn't been touched, several of the others had been shelled, predominantly with duds. These guys couldn't even put a decent coup together, which was a good thing for Beatrice.

"Actually, that action of shutting down her phone may have just saved her." The Navy tech appeared to be wholly unflappable.

"What do you mean?"

She remained at her station and started drawing on her screen with a lightpen. It showed up on the big screen and was automatically repeated in the Situation Room.

"We know they're in this general area, here." She drew far too big a circle. There were thousands of human body heat signatures in that circle.

"I've been following this vehicle." She circled it. "And this one." She circled another. "Here are their prior tracks." She turned on long white lines that snaked back and forth along the streets. He looked at the time stamps along the way. They weren't moving fast like the prior tacticals.

They were quartering the area. They'd picked up on her cell phone's signal as it tried to find a cell tower to hook up to, and they'd been triangulating in on it. They were close, less than a quarter mile to the east and south. Another few minutes and they'd have had her pinned down.

He rested his forehead on the table. He was the one who wasn't going to survive this.

Chapter 21

*T*he information *started fast*, then got faster. Navy divers had been attacked in Panama Harbor. To get beneath the range of grenades dropped into the water, they'd dived well below the limits of their breathing gear, then come up directly under Noriega's gunboat to attach the scuttling charges.

A SEAL team had taken out Noriega's private jet, cutting off that line of escape, but at a terrible loss of life. The Pineapple wasn't there, nor in his palace.

Beatrice had been allowed a corner of the 160th's control center. When the first helicopter was shot down over the marshes near the mouth of the Canal, the shock wave had rippled once around the room and been gone. She'd had lunch with "Sonny" Owen and John Hunter just last week. The guys in this room had trained with them for years. Now they were dead.

The 160th's air mission commanders were in active combat, too busy to grieve now. That would have to come later. But with little to do until the hunt for the Pineapple became a primary focus, all she could do was sit and think how Frank would feel if she died. Snuffed out in seconds, shot out of the sky. Especially with how they'd left things back on July 3rd.

It had been weeks before she'd discovered the pendant. Her key ring always had too many keys. Her place, her parent's, her sister's, the car, Frank's old place... they were always accumulating faster than she could shed them.

At some point, on that single San Antonio day, while he'd had her keys, he'd slipped a small pendant onto the ring. It was a tiny, silvered firework explosion, no bigger than her thumbnail. He'd purchased and given her an anniversary present. A thoughtful, funny one. The anniversary of his final carjacking attempt. And she hadn't even remembered the date.

She listened to the next report coming in. They'd rescued an American from nine months' solitary confinement in a maximum-security prison. It had taken four small helicopters transporting a lot of Delta Force operators and a couple more attack versions of the Little Birds flying as armed guards. On the way out, the commanding officer had taken a round that shattered his arm and lodged deep inside his right lung. She knew him best of all. She saw them land right outside the command and control center.

One of the Delta Operators jumped off his narrow bench where he'd ridden on the outside of the helicopter. They all bristled with weapons: pistols, rifles, knives, bolt cutters, explosive packs. The D-boy had slapped the commander on the arm in celebration of the mission. The commander screamed and cursed. The medics finally realized what had happened and rushed forward.

Beat wasn't in harm's way. She was a back-of-the-line consultant. But what if she weren't.

She took the little firework pendant off her key ring and hung it from the thin gold chain her sister had given her the day she'd become a Secret Service agent. The only jewelry she ever wore, until now. Now if she were killed and they found her personal effects, Frank would know she'd accepted the gift.

The rest of it she'd have to think about after they took down the Noriega.

Chapter 22

Frank: Now

I have an idea."

General Rogers returned to his chair in the Situation Room so that Frank could see his face. He had a fresh cup of coffee and red-rimmed eyes.

Frank expected he looked far worse. Even the unflappable tech was drooping in her chair. Fourteen hours since the first report that something was wrong, now barely two hours remained until daybreak in Guinea-Bissau. The fighting in the city center had peaked an hour ago and was tapering off.

Still no word from inside the country. The Guinea-Bissau ambassador had holed up in his office and refused to answer his locked door, though they knew he was in there. It was hard to blame him. He had family there who might not survive the night. And if things went the wrong way, it was possible that he could never even go home to be sure.

Based on the pattern of destruction of selected high-value homes, it appeared that the faction presently winning was not friendly to the U.S. in general. If they finished their task before darkness fell tomorrow night, they'd go hunting three Americans lost in a strange city with no resources but Beatrice Belfour's brains and stamina.

That meant they needed a solution within the remaining two hours of darkness.

How many movies had Beat dragged him to over the years where all they needed was two hours? The end of the world, *just give me two hours and I can save humanity.* Can't find true love, *in two hours I'll make her see what true love really is.* Need to save some woman's ass from the center of an African coup…

"Go ahead, Frank. What's the idea?"

"How close is the carrier group?"

"Two hundred miles. About eight minutes with an F-18 Hornet."

"They won't do me any good. Anything that lands at that airport is going to get itself shot up. Anyone around from SOAR?"

"Two DAP Hawks and three Little Birds," the Special Forces captain along the left wall chimed in. "They've been assisting on the anti-Nigerian piracy force, Operation Sure Seas. We have another company of them off Somali on the same Operation."

Two DAP Hawks? The Direct Action Penetrators were exceptionally rare birds, the nastiest Black Hawk helicopters ever put into the night sky. There were barely a dozen of them flying anywhere in the world, all flown by the Night Stalkers. What were the chances?

"Henderson and Beale?"

"It's them." General Rogers knew them well also, he'd once threatened Beale's father with fisticuffs, only half-jokingly, for the right to give away the bride at her wedding. Beale was the sort of person you'd do that for.

Frank smiled. It was the first good news he'd had since finding out Beat was alive. Her life expectancy had just jumped by a significant factor.

"Get them airborne. And one of those Stratotankers you have parked out at Cape Verde. They'll need refueling."

"Roger that. They can be on site in about an hour."

"Have them burn it hard. We're running out of darkness."

Frank thought quickly about how to make this work. Since the helicopters wouldn't know Beat's location, he needed a way for Beat to come to the helicopters.

"And General, there's one thing we need to make sure the DAP Hawks are fitted with before they start out."

# # #

Beat still lay against the stones of the goat pen wall. She was tapped. For an hour since the plane exploded she'd tried to come up some alternate plan. Charlotte had recovered enough to sit up and lean her head against Sam's chest and weep quietly.

The ambassador had the decency to assure her they were going to get married as soon as they got back stateside, even if he had to roust a judge out of bed. Beat and Sam Green both knew their chances were not good and diminishing with every passing minute.

She'd try hiding them again. Would find the energy in another few minutes to give it one last effort, but she'd now been awake for two days, running, hiding, and battered. Her ears were still ringing, in fact ringing was all her left ear was giving her. Her directional hearing didn't exist at the moment.

Hearing.

There was a sound in the night. It was an odd sound. Like an oversized washing machine or a…

"Sam, where's that sound coming from?"

"What sound?" But he was turning his head one way and another hunting for it, so she kept quiet. He glanced up more than once, but couldn't seem to locate it.

Then she knew.

"Okay, everyone this is it. Get ready for one last effort."

"This is what?"

Beat blessed her association with the 160th SOAR that had started all the way back in Panama in 1989. She'd kept up with them, made sure she was a contact point when they needed a liaison for a diplomatic security mission. She hadn't ridden with them but once, and that hadn't been combat, real or simulated. Damn but she'd been envious when Frank got that training ride last winter. Well, maybe this was her chance.

Please let it be her chance.

"That's a stealth U.S. Special Forces Black Hawk helicopter. The same kind that went into Osama bin Laden's compound. That's why you hear them, but you can't tell where the sound is coming from. Now all we have to do is figure out where they're expecting to find us and get there."

"Where's that?"

"Damned if I know."

Then she heard the sound, blaring out of the sky. She watched which way Sam and Charlotte's heads turned, the choppers were to the south of them, deeper into the city than she'd dared go. It was music. Unlike the odd sound of the stealth helicopters rotors, that often sounded as if they were flying away when they were actually coming right at you, the music would be intensely directional. It would blast from a loudspeaker attached to the chopper and tell bad guys exactly where to aim.

It was music she knew well. It informed her that Frank Adams was involved and looking out for her. The sudden relief so sharp she wanted to cry.

He'd absolutely known what to play. It was the only movie series where she'd dragged him to the opening night of every sequel. She had a weak spot for Tom Cruise. And the *Mission Impossible* theme echoing through the pre-dawn darkness of Bissau city, told her that the message was for her and she'd better listen and listen hard.

# # #

"But that doesn't make any sense." The President was back in the U.S. Security Center in the U.N.'s basement. Hank was still at the table and General Rogers was still on the screen. The President was looking at the script John had just recorded and sent to the choppers for playback.

"Trust me, Mr. President, it makes perfect sense. It's at least a triple letter score, and I'm prayin' plenty hard that it's a triple word score." Frank knew it would work. It just had to. If Beat Belfour was still alive in the city, she'd get there.

He just hoped to god she was still mobile. Because they had no way to go find her, she had to find them.

"Major Beale?"

"Here Frank." The right-hand screen was now showing a four-segment feed from the DAP Hawk helicopter as she now circled over the city. The screen was cut up into quarters and showed what Beale saw as she turned her helmet, the ghostly gray images of the ADAS cameras they'd installed six months earlier that showed the nighttime city in the stark imagery of a black-and-white movie as bright as daylight. The other three segments on the screen were views from the belly of the chopper, ahead, and to either side. Bissau was laid out before them.

"I think we've played the music long enough to get her attention. I need you to circle slowly enough that she can hear a full set of instructions."

"Just reminding you that these people have surface-to-air missiles. Slow wouldn't be my first choice."

"Okay, uh," Frank thought quickly. Thought about how Beat had attacked him at the Federal Law Enforcement Training Center—fast repeated attack of his body.

"How about multiple faster passes? Let her pick up the segments as she needs them."

"Roger that."

Typical Major Beale and typical SOAR. A two word acknowledge before flying into a hot battle zone.

"Switch over to message broadcast."

"Switching."

Frank heard his own voice, picked up faintly through Beale's microphone.

"Beat your ass. Start where…"

# # #

Beatrice laughed and had to muffle her mouth in her *dashiki* to hide it. She almost missed the first instruction.

"Beat, your ass." Was one of the compliments that Frank had paid her the very first time they'd made love in the woods on that Georgia night at FLETC. It had been in an awed, breathy whisper, the memory of which could heat her blood even now. He'd made a real thing about cupping her behind in those powerful hands of his to pull her against him. No question about the authenticity of this message.

And he'd also told her to that they had to "beat their asses" if this was going to work. Time to move fast.

Start where Bruce fought the second time, the time after the tower.

Sam Green started to ask her what that meant, but she shushed him so that she could listen. She started to translate to him in whispers as she waited for that message to repeat several times.

"Bruce Willis, *Die Hard 2*, the second movie. The first time he fought in a tower, a skyscraper, the Nakatomi Plaza. Otherwise it might have been Bruce Lee, who fought in a temple. The second time Bruce Willis fought, it was in an airport. That's our starting frame of reference." It was perfect. No one, who didn't have their common ground of going to so many movies, would be able to follow these directions.

Go the direction Cary and Eva Marie didn't go.

"They're fading away," Charlotte's whisper was panicked.

It was true. The chopper circling out toward the airport, too far away to hear the next instruction.

"It doesn't matter, they'll be back."

"But what did it mean?" Sam helped Charlotte to her feet as Beatrice rose. Her side had stiffened badly and she had definitely sprained her right knee when she dove out of the plane. She just hoped she hadn't torn anything. She ran a quick hand over her leg down the outside of the *dashiki*. Definitely swollen. Swollen badly, but it still took her weight.

"It means that we're in the wrong neighborhood." She led them off into the night. Cary Grant and Eva Marie Saint had been chased all over the landscape of Mount Rushmore in *North by Northwest*. "Go the way they didn't go." She needed to be south-southeast of the airport.

One hour to first light. She ignored her knee and got them moving. They had to hurry.

# # #

"We're starting to pick up some fire," Major Mark Henderson's voice remained absolutely calm. "Request permission to engage." It even sounded as if he was looking forward to it. As pilot of the second DAP Hawk, he'd be flying as backup wingman to his wife commanding the primary rescue bird.

The President and Frank looked at each other. The situation was escalating. G-B military forces had finally noticed that there were helicopters circling overhead. Hard to miss, even if they would have trouble locating them. The airport's radar should be useless against the stealth modifications. They would appear as flickers no bigger than a large bird, and never quite in the location where they actually were.

The problem was that most of the anti-electronic warfare defenses they carried, the ones that scrambled sophisticated tracking-and-homing equipment, were useless. The G-B army didn't have the high-end detection gear or automated aim and fire anti-aircraft. They had fifty-year-old Russian cannons that were aimed by hand and fired one inch shells. Rifles, rocket-propelled-grenade launchers produced in Brazil and left behind by the Portuguese when they left in the 1970s, five-inch howitzers. The weapons were so unsophisticated that they actually posed a considerable threat.

"Major Henderson. This is President Matthews."

"Hello, sir. How's the poker coming along?"

"Smart enough to not play you the next time you're in town."

That got a laugh. They all knew that the President would play anyway and didn't really care that he rarely won. It had also given him the moment to make sure his thoughts were clear.

"Yes. You are hereby authorized to use limited force, only as necessary, to ensure the security of this operation. Discretion is yours."

"Roger that, sir."

Even as Henderson spoke, a sharp hiss sounded in the background. Frank recognized it as one of the FFAR rockets mounted in pods on the sides of the DAP Hawk. Through Major Beale's view, they could see the rocket streak downward from her husband's otherwise invisible helicopter.

It impacted an armored vehicle with a multi-rocket launcher mounted on its roof. It was visible for just an instant before it disappeared in a massive fireball when all of the unfired rockets exploded simultaneously sending a huge ball of fire skyward.

"I guess they know we're here now." Mark didn't sound the least contrite.

They went back to their circling, Major Beale continued her broadcast.

Chapter 23

Beat: H-Hour plus three days, 1989

B*eat flew with SOAR.* They had her in the back of one of the big twin-rotor Chinook helicopters. It was filled with the roar of the massive twin turbines and the sharp, stinging scent of kerosene from the Jet A fuel. Other than the red, night-time lights in the long cargo bay, there was little to see. Even pressing her face to the glass of the small round windows only revealed the stars.

She spent most of the trip sitting on a giant rubber bladder filled with fuel. Cases of rockets and ammunition were stacked at the front of the cargo bay.

She was sitting in a flying bomb.

All of this was part of a FARP, a Forward Arming and Refueling Point. Their destination was too far away for the Little Birds and Black Hawks to make the round trip. They were flying from Panama City down to the Colombian border as part of the Hunt for Elvis. That's what the Special Forces operators, showing a little more imagination, had renamed the hunt for the Pineapple. Noriega had remained elusive right into day three of the taking of Panama, three days without a single sighting, as rare as Elvis.

They'd gotten a report of a jungle hideaway he often used down near the Colombian border. It was expected to be a dry hole, no one home, or they probably wouldn't have let her come along. But they'd wanted her expertise on hidden security systems and possible hideaways.

"Engaging now," the pilot announced over the intercom. There was nothing to see or hear, their chopper was five miles behind the others. They were here for resupply, not part of the battle. Though the crew didn't act that way. In addition to the four crew chiefs ready to reload and refuel any helicopter, there were the two pilots up front, a pair of chiefs manning M60 machine guns mounted in side-opening windows. The big rear tail ramp had been lowered and a chief wearing a harness, in case he fell during radical maneuvers, stood at the end of the ramp manning another large gun.

The announcements by the pilot occurred on about a thirty-second pulse revealing again how practiced these guys were.

"First team in."

"Security guards down."

She fingered her fireworks pendant and wondered what had led her to run from Brooklyn to Fort Sam Houston, and from there to the Panamanian jungle.

"Perimeter secure."

In some odd way, unable to witness what was occurring in the nearby jungle, she was finally able to see her own actions from a distance.

"Inside cleared. Appears to be a dry hole."

That was her cue. The Chinook nosed down and roared forward. They'd search the place for any intelligence and possible hiding places, but he wasn't here.

Neither Elvis nor Frank Adams.

Chapter 24

Beat: Now

*T*hree times the length *of Kate and Leo's boat.*

And what part of Frank's thick head thought she'd remember the length of the *Titanic?*

The three of them were sprinting from shadow to shadow just one block west of the Beast in Bandim road. It was almost perfectly south-southeast of the main airport terminal. But tanks and tacticals were roaring up and down the main road.

At each intersection she'd wait and listen. Listen for the roaring of diesel engines, the high-whine and grinding gears of the pickups. When there was a break, they'd jump the gap and move farther from the airport.

And the idiot assumed that she knew exactly where they were from the airport. Like she'd be carrying a tape measure with her.

Wait, he'd know that. He'd know that she could only approximate. The *Titanic* was way longer than five-hundred feet and definitely less than a thousand. Times three. Call it a third to a half mile. That she could manage and kept heading south by southeast. They still had a ways to go.

Follow Witherspoon and get Blonde.

She froze and Sam and Charlotte actually ran into her.

She leaned against a wall, first light couldn't be more than fifteen minutes off. In the tropics that meant daybreak within half an hour.

And they'd be dead an hour after that.

At the most.

"Idiot." She hissed out.

"What?" Sam and Charlotte did their best to shrink into the shadow with her.

A chopper flew overhead heading north fast. Gunfire followed it. Handguns, rifles, and the sharp bark of a tactical's big machine gun spewing out ten rounds a second.

"I don't know that reference."

"Which?"

"*Legally Blonde.* I had the flu and never much liked Reese Witherspoon anyway. He went by himself."

"*Legally Blonde.* Cute movie," Charlotte gasped, desperately trying to catch her breath and speak at the same time. "She's all blonde. And empty-headed. Or so everyone thinks. Including her really crappy ex-boyfriend."

All of the clues had been about places. "What's the setting?"

"Harvard Law School."

Sam pointed down the road. "There's a University about a dozen blocks that way." His breathing wasn't much better than his lover's, or Beat's own.

"Big empty lot across the street from the school. I think. I was taken there once, tour of the country's progress. It wasn't much, but it was a university."

"That's it. Last stretch." She got them running again. Had never reached so deep, hadn't even known she had reserves that went that far, but she did it. And this had better be it, because it was the last stretch for all three of them.

# # #

"That's them. Has to be." The tech called out.

Major Emily Beale flew fast over something which was such a blur on the screen that Frank hadn't registered anything unusual.

The tech had seen it though. She pulled up the image on the central screen and revealed three figures ducking from house to house, cautiously moving south. So close, but there was no way for the helicopter to get in among the huts and houses to fetch them. Everything was too tightly packed. They needed the open field of at least sixty-feet across for the Black Hawk's rotors.

"This doesn't look good." Major Henderson announced and the tech picked up his helmet camera's view and set it over General Rogers' image on the feed from the Situation Room.

The battle for the center of the city had run its course. Tanks and APCs, armored personnel carriers, were moving onto the Fera di Bandim road. They'd be hurrying out to the airport to secure the most significant asset of the country other than the downtown and the port. Indeed some of the traffic turned and raced to reinforce the port, but the bulk of it was heading their way.

And at the rate Beat and the others were moving, they'd reach the empty lot at about the same time as the bulk of the Guinea-Bissau army. There was no way to tell which faction had won and they couldn't risk waiting to find out.

"Beale!" Frank shouted. "Put me direct to the speakers."

He yelled out a command.

# # #

Beat heard Frank's voice roar out of the sky.

It was so loud, the helicopter flew low and fast directly overhead, that it took her a moment to unravel the words from the sheer blast of volume.

Neo! Take the red pill! Now!

The Matrix. Take the pill of the harsh reality.

"Run!" she yelled at Sam and Charlotte.

She pulled out her pistol and shoved them so hard they almost landed on their faces.

A local looked out their hut door to see what was going on and she fired a shot into the top of the door frame.

They ducked back inside.

As they sprinted, Beat heard the chopper swing over them again. It slowed enough to hover just behind them.

A blast of downdraft shoved at their backs.

She glanced back and saw that a cloud of dust boiled upward beneath the rotor blades. Anyone attempting to follow them would be blinded and choked by the brownout.

A glance up and she could see the bright sparks of small weapon's fire pinging off the hull.

With a brap like a dragon's roar, the hovering chopper opened up with their mini-guns. These weren't the big machine guns on the tacticals firing five hundred rounds-a-minute. The M134 six-barrel Gatling guns rained down lead at eighty rounds-a-second.

They looked like a dark-red whip of God, right on the very edge of vision, but bright in the night-vision gear the chopper crew would be wearing. Twin streams of hell swirled and slashed down from the heavens and across the street behind them and to either side. Anyone stupid enough to fire at the chopper wouldn't last long under such an onslaught.

Something exploded. A car. A truck. She didn't wait to see.

With a shove against their backs, she got Sam and Charlotte moving even faster. Another local in a doorway to her right, this time with a rifle.

Her first shot drilled him in the forehead, the second in the heart before he even knew he was dead. They were past him before he even had time to collapse.

A second helicopter swooped low, passing through the raking gunfire from the ground and dropping down to street level a hundred feet ahead of them.

They'd reached the empty lot.

The two crewmen on the miniguns were pouring lead back over Beat's head so hard and close she could feel the heat of their passage.

She clapped a hand on Sam's and Charlotte's heads to keep them below the swing of the rotors and the slash of the gunfire.

They dove through the wide-open door of the Black Hawk's cargo bay in unison, almost tumbling out the far side with their momentum.

Charlotte screamed, and the chopper roared as it clawed back into the sky.

Several FFAR rockets sizzled from the other helicopter in rapid formation and then a Hellfire missile roared down into the road. The nasty war cry of its rocket motor like nothing else in the sky.

The shockwave knocked their own chopper aside as they scrambled for distance. A hand on her back was all that kept her from tumbling out the door as the helicopter struggled through the turbulence, and then, as suddenly as a light switch being thrown, they were above it.

A glance down at the fast receding ground showed a massive crater in the middle of the main road. Parts of a tank burned in the center of the crater even as another tank drove right in on top of it. People began pouring out of the hatches even as it too began to burn.

The hand on her back that had saved her belonged to one of the crew chiefs.

"Just the three of you?" A woman. The gunner was a woman. How cool was that?

Beat nodded, it was all she had the breath for.

The choppers climbed into the lightening sky. Within moments they cleared the city. Before Beat could even think clearly that she'd survived, they were passing over wide mangrove swamps and finally off the coast.

As they climbed toward a refueling tanker, Guinea-Bissau was certainly a place she was glad to be leaving behind.

"You know that you're bleeding?"

She knew that her knee hurt like hell. Twisted, maybe torn. And her ribs, she'd escalated her assessment from sore to cracked.

It was only when the woman took her arm that Beat hissed with pain. The crew chief pulled out a long knife and carefully slit the bloody *dashiki* then folded it back from Beat's arm. A long scrape from shoulder to elbow, a graze that had removed a narrow line of skin before continuing on its way.

Beat turned to look at the others. Sam was sitting on the deck, still had his burlap sack tied across his back. Charlotte lay with her head in his lap as the other crew chief was binding her leg. Charlotte had pressed her lips white, but she was being brave about having a hole shot in her thigh.

Charlotte gave them both a thumb's up which were returned with thankful nods.

The crew woman who'd just finished bandaging her arm tapped her on the good shoulder.

"Welcome aboard. I'm Connie Davis. That's Kee Smith helping your friends. There's someone who wants to speak to you." Connie was holding out a headset.

Beat pulled it on.

"Beatrice Belfour here."

"So," she knew that rumbling voice better than she knew her own. "So," she could hear the smile and the relief as Frank Adams repeated himself.

"So, you've got skills."

Six Days and Seven Nights. She'd escaped the pirates alive because both she and Frank had skills.

"I've got skills." She closed her eyes against the brightness of the rising sun and listened to his gentle laugh.

"You'll be at the airport?" She had to know.

"I'll be there."

And he would be.

"I didn't get you a present."

It would be their anniversary. This was July third, she'd probably be landing back at Dulles or Andrews Air Force on the fourth.

"You never remember."

And she didn't. But she still wore the little silver firework around her neck as her only jewelry after twenty-five years together.

"But I'll be there."

And he always had been. After every single mission she'd returned from since Panama, he'd been waiting for her at the airport gate.

She'd radioed him from Panama City after they'd taken Noriega. He'd given himself up at the gates of the Vatican embassy and they'd shipped him to the U.S. for trial and incarceration.

Beatrice had asked Frank to be there in San Antonio and he had been. She'd asked him to marry her as she stepped off the jetway and into his arms. He hadn't even let her leave the airport. He'd bundled her on a plane for Reno and married her later that day because he didn't want her to get away. It had been plenty romantic. Though after the hunt for Noriega, she'd turned down his repeated offer to have Elvis be best man.

"I'll be there for you," his voice the sweetest sound Beatrice Ann Belfour had ever heard.

"And I for you." The words she'd promised that day from a country in flames to the man she loved.

A promise they'd both kept ever since.

About the Author

M. L. *Buchman's romances* have been named Booklist Top 10 of the year and NPR Top 5 of the year. He also has published both science fiction and fantasy under the name Matthew Lieber Buchman and a foodie thriller as Matthew J. Booker. He is happiest, no matter how cliché it may seem, when walking on the beach holding hands with the mother of his awesome kid… or when he's writing. In among his career as a corporate project manager, he has rebuilt and single-handed a fifty-foot sailboat, both flown and jumped out of airplanes, designed and built two houses, and bicycled solo around the world. He is now making his living full-time as a writer, living on the Oregon Coast. You may keep up with his writing at www.mlbuchman.com.

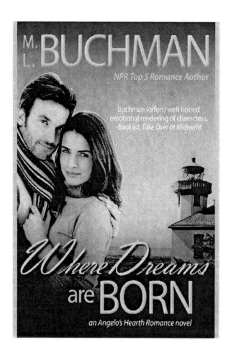

Where Dreams Are Born (excerpt)

R*ussell locked his door* as the last of the staff finally went home and turned off his camera.

He knew it was good. The images were there, solid. He'd really captured them.

But something was missing.

The groove ran so clean when he slid into it. The studio faded into the background, then the strobe lights, reflector umbrellas, and blue and green backdrops all became texture and tone.

Image, camera, man became one and they were all that mattered; a single flow of light beginning before time was counted and ending in the printed image. A ray of primordial light traveling forever to glisten off the BMW roadster still parked in one corner of the wood-planked studio. Another ray lost in the dark blackness of the finest leather bucket seats. One more picking out the supermodel's perfect hand dangling a single, shining, golden key. The image shot just slow enough that they key blurred as it spun, but the logo remained clear.

He couldn't quite put his finger on it…

Another great ad by Russell Morgan. Russell Morgan, Inc. The client would be knocked dead, and the ad leaving all others standing still as it roared down the passing lane. Might get him another Clio, or even a second Mobius.

But… There wasn't usually a "but." The groove had definitely been there, but he hadn't been in it. That was the problem. It had slid along, sweeping his staff into their own orchestrated perfection, but he'd remained untouched. Not part of that ideal, seamless flow.

"Be honest, boyo, that session sucked," he told the empty studio. Everything had come together so perfectly for yet another ad for yet another high-end glossy. *Man, the Magazine* would launch spectacularly in a few weeks, a high-profile mid-December launch, a never before seen twelve page spread by Russell Morgan, Inc. and the rag would probably never pay off the lavish launch party of hope, ice sculptures, and chilled magnums of champagne before disappearing like a thousand before it.

He stowed the last camera he'd been using with the others piled by his computer. At the breaker box he shut off the umbrellas, spots, scoops, and washes. The studio shifted from a stark landscape in hard-edged relief to a nest of curious shadows and rounded forms. The tang of hot metal and deodorant were the only lasting result of the day's efforts.

"Morose tonight, aren't we?" he asked his reflection in the darkened window of his Manhattan studio. His reflection was wise enough to not answer back. There wasn't ever a "down" after a shoot, there had always been an "up."

Not tonight.

He'd kept everyone late, even though it was Thanksgiving eve, hoping for that smooth slide of image, camera, man. It was only when he saw the power of the images he captured that he knew he wasn't a part of the chain anymore and decided he'd paid enough triple-time expenses.

The single perfect leg wrapped in thigh-high red-leather boots visible in the driver's seat. The sensual juxtaposition of woman and sleek machine. An ad designed to wrap every person with even a hint of a Y-chromosome around its little finger. And those with only X-chromosomes would simply want to be her. A perfect combo of sex for the guys and power for the women.

Russell had become no more than the observer, the technician behind the camera. Now that he faced it, months, maybe even a year had passed since he'd been yanked all the way into the light-image-camera-man slipstream. Tonight was the first time he hadn't even trailed in the churned up wake.

"You're just a creative cog in the advertising photography machine." Ouch! That one stung, but it didn't turn aside the relentless steamroller of his thoughts speeding down some empty, godforsaken autobahn.

His career was roaring ahead, his business fast and smooth, but, now that he considered it, he really didn't give a damn.

His life looked perfect, but—"Don't think it!" —but his autobahn mind finished, "it wasn't."

Russell left his silent reflection to its own thoughts and went through the back door that led to his apartment, closing it tightly on the perfect BMW, the perfect rose on the seat, and somewhere, lost among a hundred other props from dozens of other shoots, the long pair of perfect red-leather Chanel boots that had been wrapped around the most expensive legs in Manhattan. He didn't care if he never walked back through that door again. He'd been doing his art by rote, and how God-awful sad was that?

And he shot commercial art. He'd never had the patience to do art for art's sake. No draw for him. No fire. He left the apartment dark, only a soft glow from the blind-covered windows revealing the vaguest outlines of the framed art on the wall. Even that almost overwhelmed him.

He didn't want to see the huge prints by the art artists: autographed Goldsworthy, Liebowitz, and Joseph Francis' photomosaics for the moderns. A hundred and fifty more rare, even one of a kind prints, all the way back through Bourke-White to his prize, an original Daguerre. The collection that the Museum of Modern Art kept begging to borrow for a show. He bypassed the circle of chairs and sofas that could be a playpen for two or a party for twenty. He cracked the fridge in the stainless steel and black kitchen searching for something other than his usual beer.

A bottle of Krug.

Maybe he was just being grouchy after a long day's work.

Milk.

No. He'd run his enthusiasm into the ground but good.

Juice even.

Would he miss the camera if he never picked it up again?

No reaction.

Nothing.

Not even a twinge.

That was an emptiness he did not want to face. Alone, in his apartment, in the middle of the world's most vibrant city.

Russell turned away, and just as the door swung closed, the last sliver of light, the relentless cold blue-white of the refrigerator bulb, shone across his bed. A quick grab snagged the edge of the door and left the narrow beam illuminating a long pale form on his black bedspread.

The Chanel boots weren't in the studio. They were still wrapped around those three thousand dollar-an-hour legs. The only clothing on a perfect body, five foot-eleven of intensely toned female anatomy, right down to her exquisitely stair-mastered behind. Her long, white-blond hair, a perfect Godiva over the tanned breasts. Except for their too exact symmetry, even the closest inspection didn't reveal the work done there. One leg raised just ever so slightly to hide what was meant to be revealed later. Discovered.

Melanie.

By the steady rise and fall of her flat stomach, he knew she'd fallen asleep, waiting for him to finish in the studio.

How long had they been an item? Two months? Three?

She'd made him feel alive. At least when he was with her. The image of the supermodel in his bed. On his arm at yet another SoHo gallery opening, dazzling New York's finest at another three-star restaurant, wooing another gathering of upscale people with her ever so soft, so sensual, so studied French accent. Together they were wired into the heart of the in-crowd.

But that wasn't him, was it? It didn't sound anything like the Russell he once knew.

Perhaps "they" were about how he looked on her arm?

Did she know tomorrow was the annual Thanksgiving ordeal at his parents? That he'd rather die than attend? Any number of eligible woman floating about who'd finagled an invitation in hopes of snaring one of *People Magazine*'s "100 Most Eligible." Heir to a billion or some such, but wealthy enough on his own, by his own sweat. Number twenty-four this year, up from forty-seven the year before despite Tom Cruise being available yet again.

No.

Not Melanie. It wasn't the money that drew her. She wanted him. But more, she wanted the life that came with him, wrapped in the man package. She wanted The Life. The one that People Magazine readers dreamed about between glossy pages.

His fingertips were growing cold where they held the refrigerator door cracked open.

If he woke her there'd be amazing sex. Or a great party to go to. Or…

Did he want "Or"? Did he want more from her? Sex. Companionship. An energy, a vivacity, a thirst he feared that he lacked. Yes.

But where hid that smooth synchronicity like light-image-cameraman? Where lurked that perfect flow from one person to another? Did she feel it? Could he… ever again?

"More?" he whispered into the darkness to test the sound.

The door slid shut, escaped from numb fingers, plunging the apartment back into darkness, taking Melanie along with it.

His breath echoed in the vast darkness. Proof that he was alive, if nothing more.

Time to close the studio. Time to be done with Russell Incorporated. Then what?

Maybe Angelo would know what to do. He always claimed he did. Maybe this time Russell would actually listen to his almost-brother, though he knew from the experience of being himself for the last thirty years that was unlikely. Seattle. Damn! He'd have to go to bloody Seattle to find his best friend.

He could guarantee that wouldn't be a big hit with Melanie.

Now if he only knew if that was a good thing or bad.

# # #

JANUARY 1

If you were still alive, you'd pay for this one, Daddy." The moment the words escaped her lips, Cassidy Knowles slapped a hand over her mouth to negate them, but it was too late.

The sharp wind took her words and threw them back into the pine trees, guilt and all. It might have stopped her, if it didn't make this the hundredth time she'd cursed him this morning.

She leaned into the wind and forged her way downhill until the muddy path broke free from the mossy smell of the trees. Her Stuart Weitzman boots were long since soaked through, and now her feet were freezing. The two-inch heels had nearly flipped her into the mud a dozen different times.

Cassidy Knowles stared at the lighthouse. It perched upon a point of rock, tall and white, with its red roof as straight and snug as a prim bonnet. A narrow trail traced along the top of the breakwater leading to the lighthouse. The parking lot, much to her chagrin, was empty; six, beautiful, empty spaces.

"Sorry, ma'am," park rangers were always polite when telling you what you couldn't do. "The parking lot by the light is reserved for physically-challenged visitors only. You'll have to park here. It is just a short walk to the lighthouse."

The fact that she was dressed for a nice afternoon lunch at Pike Place Market safe in Seattle's downtown rather than a blustery mile-long walk on the first day of the year didn't phase the ranger in the slightest.

Cassidy should have gone home, would have, if it hadn't been for the letter stuffed deep in her pocket. So, instead of a tasty treat in a cozy deli, she'd buttoned the top button of her suede Bernardo jacket and headed down the trail. At least the promised rain had yet to arrive, so the jacket was only cold, not wet. The stylish cut had never been intended to fight off the bajillion mile-an-hour gusts that snapped it painfully against her legs. And her black leggings ranged about five layers short of tolerable and a far, far cry from warm.

At the lighthouse, any part of her that had been merely numb slipped right over to quick frozen. Leaning into the wind to stay upright, tears streaming from her eyes, she could think of a thing or two to tell her father despite his recent demise and her general feelings about the usefulness of upbraiding a dead man.

"What a stupid present!" the wind tore her shout word-by-word, syllable-by-syllable and sent flying back toward her nice warm car and the smug park ranger.

A calendar. He'd given her a stupid calendar of stupid lighthouses and a stupid letter to open at each stupid one. He'd been very insistent, made her promise. One she couldn't ignore. A deathbed promise.

Cassidy leaned grimly forward to start walking only to have the wind abruptly cease. She staggered, nearly planting her face on the pavement before another gust sent her crabbing sideways. With resolute force, she planted one foot after another until she'd crossed that absolutely vacant parking lot with its six empty spaces and staggered along the top of the breakwater to reach the lighthouse itself. No handicapped people crazy enough to come here New Year's morning. No people at all for that matter.

The building's wall was concrete, worn smooth by a thousand storms and a hundred coats of brilliant white paint. With the wind practically pinning her to the outside of the building, she peeked into one of the windows. The wind blew her hair about so that it beat on her eyes and mouth trying to simultaneously blind and choke her. With one hand, she grabbed the unruly mass mostly to one side. With the other she shaded the dusty window. The cobwebbed glass revealed an equally unkempt interior.

No lightkeeper sitting in his rocking chair before a merry fire. No smoking pipe. No lighthouse cat curled in his lap. Some sort of a rusty engine not attached to anything. A bucket of old tools. A couple of paint cans.

A high wave crashed into the rocks with a thundering shudder that ran up through the heels of her boots and whipped a chill spray into the wind. Salt water on suede.

Daddy now owed her a new coat as well.

Cassidy edged along the foundation until she found a calmer spot, a bit of windshadow behind the lighthouse where the wind chill ranked merely miserable rather than horrific on the suck-o-meter. Squatting down behind one of the breakwater's boulders helped a tiny bit more. She peeled off her thin leather gloves and blew against her fingertips to warm them enough so that they'd work. Once she'd regained some modicum of feeling, she pulled out the letter.

She couldn't feel his writing, though she ran her fingertips over it again and again. His Christmas present. A five-dollar calendar of Washington lighthouses from the hospital gift store and a dozen thin envelopes wrapped in a old x-ray folder with no ribbon, no paper.

In the end he'd foiled her final Christmas hunt. It had been her great yearly quest. The ultimate grail of childhood, finding the key present before Christmas morning. There was no present he could hide that she couldn't find. Not the Cabbage Patch Kid when she was six; the one she'd had to hold with her arm in a cast, from falling off the kitchen stool she'd dragged into her father's closet. Not the used VW Rabbit he'd hidden out in the wine shed thinking that she never went there anymore.

And she didn't, except for some reason the day before her eighteenth Christmas.

A part of her wanted to crumple the letter up and throw it into the sea. It was too soon. She didn't want to face the pain again.

Too soon.

The rest of her did what it supposed to do. The dutiful daughter opened the envelope and pinned the letter against her thigh so that she could read the slashing scrawl that was her father's. Even as weak with sickness as he must have been, it looked scribed in stone. His bold-stroke writing gave the words a force and strength just as his deep voice had once sounded strong enough to keep the world at bay for his small girl.

> *Dearest Ice Sweet,*

He'd always called her that.

Icewine. The grapes traditionally harvested on her birthday, December twenty-first. "The sweetest wine of all, my little ice sweet girl." By the age of five she knew about the sugar content of icewine, Riesling, Chardonnay, and a dozen others. By eight she could identify scores of vintages just by the scent of the cork and hundreds by their logos though she'd yet to taste more than thimblefuls of watered wine at any one time.

Cassidy stared at the waves digging angrily at the rocks. Spray slashed sideways by the wind dragged tears from her eyes even as she struggled to blink them dry. She hadn't cried in a long time and she was damned if she was going to start now simply because she was cold and there was a hole in her heart.

Seven days. She'd looked away for a one moment seven days ago and he was gone. Christmas morning. He'd hung on long enough to tell her of his last present, hidden in plain sight in the used X-ray folder on the side table. A long list of crossed-out names had shuttled films back and forth across Northwest Hospital. Last used by someone named Barash. No meaning for her whatsoever.

> *I bought this calendar the day you moved back to Seattle. Marked in all the "dates." Now I know that I won't get to go with you. I'm sorry to leave you so young.*

"I'm twenty-nine, Daddy." But it felt young. Her birthday gone unremarked because he'd never woken that day so close to his last. The hole in her heart was so broad that it would never be filled.

He'd only been gone a week. Cremated, waked, and ashes spread on his beloved vineyard by the permission of the new owners. They'd owned his vineyard for five years, but still, they were the new ones. It still wasn't right, them living in the place where her father belonged. She could still picture him striding among the vines, rubbing the soil in his palm, showing his only child the wonders of the changing seasons, the lifecycle of a grapevine, and the nurturing of honeybees.

> *For our first "date" I will just tell you how proud I am of you. My daughter took a vintner's education and turned herself into the best food-and-wine columnist ever.*

He always believed in her. Always rooted for her. Always cheered her on. He'd been the same way with her boyfriends. Always welcoming them when they arrived. Always consoling her when they were gone. No judgment, not even on the ones she should have avoided like a bottle of rotgut Thunderbird.

The wind rattled the paper sharply, drawing her attention back to the letter.

> *You are so like me. You figure out what feels right and you just go do it, damn the consequences. I could never fault you for leaving. I always did what I wanted, too. Saw it and went right for it, no discussion needed. All the while wearing perfect blinders that blocked out everything else. You got that from me. You come by your whimsical stubbornness honestly, Ice Sweet.*

She wasn't stubborn, years of careful planning had led her this far. Even her move to Seattle to be with him had been calculated, though she never told him about that. She shifted on the hard rock that was in imminent danger of freezing her butt.

Her father kept apologizing for all the wrong things. Seattle had ended up being a great career move, or was becoming one as she'd hoped. In New York, she had worked as one of a thousand food and wine reviewers. Okay one in fifty, maybe even one in twenty-five, she was damn good, but there were only three women at that level. The other twenty-two were members of longstanding in the old boys' club.

"We're looking for someone with a more refined palate." Read as someone who was "male."

She'd let go of her sublet in Manhattan when she'd found out he was sick. Bought a condo in Seattle to be near, but not too near him on Bainbridge Island. Helped him move into the elder-care by Northgate when he couldn't care for himself any longer, and from there to Northwest Hospital where she'd lived out his last two weeks in the chair by his bed.

The *Village Voice* dropped her the day she left Manhattan. That had hurt as they'd run her first-ever review, a short piece on Jim and Charlie's Punk and Wine Bistro. Jim and Charlie's was still there, partly thanks to that review that was still framed and hung in the center of the bar's mirror.

But in Seattle she was rapidly rising to the very upper crust of the apple pie. Her reviews ran in every local paper. The *San Francisco Chronicle* had picked her up for their Travel section the following week making it difficult to stay grumpy about the loss of The Voice. Then AAA took her national with their magazines. From there, it hadn't been a big step to national syndication. Six more months in New York and she'd have still been grinding her way up from the twentieth spot to the nineteenth. She was going to bypass the lot of them by skipping right past the de rigueur hurdles and sitting at the head table herself.

Her father's cancer had brought at least that much good. Now if only it hadn't taken him with it.

And she wasn't whimsical, no matter what he thought. Her dad had always described her mother as the organized one. And Cassidy had done her best to be just like her. You didn't become a topcolumnist by following the wind all willy-nilly.

If she didn't hurry, she was going to freeze in place. She chafed at her legs with one hand and then the other, but it didn't help. She was cold past any cure less than a piping-hot tub bath. She peeked ahead, just two and a bit pages. She turned to the second sheet.

I started the vineyard after my tour in Vietnam. Got signed off the base and walked out of San Francisco right across the Golden Gate. No home, no job, no one to go back to. Headed up into the hills, don't even know why or where I was. Walked and hitched 'til dark, slept, woke with the light, and kept moving.

One morning, I woke up in a field, leaning against a rotting, wooden fencepost, looking at the saddest little vineyard you could imagine. Poor vines dying of thirst. I found an old bucket and started watering them from a nearby stream. Old man came out to lean on the fence. Watched me quite a while, a couple hours maybe. I didn't care about him. Those vines were the first thing I'd cared about in a long, long time.

"You want 'em?" the old guy asked. "Five hundred bucks and they're yours."

I don't even remember how it happened. One minute my final pay was in my pocket, then his. Other vets drifted in. I charged them fifty bucks to join. Five of us worked the land, recovered the vines. That was the start of the thirty acres of Knowles Valley Vineyard.

She'd never heard how his first vineyard started. Didn't even really know where it was, somewhere in the hills of northern California.

Though he might have ambled all the way to Oregon for how much she knew.

Walk the year with me. Let's take our time. My past is mine, but your future is not. That's only up to you. I leave you to walk alone, it is a rough trail often over rocky soil. But keep your head high and you'll go far.

Whatever happens, know that I love you. I'm so proud of you.

Love you Ice Sweet,

Vic

Vic. He always signed his letters "Vic." Never what she'd always called him. "Daddy."

"I could never fault you for leaving." Yet between the lines that's just what he did. Nothing on the backs of any of the pages. She worked to refold the pages in the wind.

"No, you're imagining things, Cass. You think too much. Get your head out of your own butt." And she mostly did. One of the many gifts

Vic Knowles had given her, the ability to be clear about her own actions and reactions.

He'd financed her dreams of getting away from the rain capital of the Pacific Northwest. He'd paid for her college in full and cooking school after that. It was only cleaning up his papers this last week that she saw how close it had come to breaking him. He'd just made it a natural assumption that she'd go to college and he'd pay. Just like her Mom who had a degree in economics from Vassar. He'd always talked about how smart Cassidy's mother was. How beautiful. How much he missed her.

He hadn't gone to college himself, not even high school. His past was little more than a few facts she'd winnowed over the years. His dad had left before he could remember. He'd dropped out of third grade to help his mother run the grocery store. They were desperately poor when she died. Then he'd gone to Vietnam at eighteen as the only way to make a living wage. And walked to a vineyard. But he gave Cassidy that gift of education as if it was no sacrifice to him.

Did he now begrudge her that past? The future he never had.

No. That didn't make any sense. He hadn't thought about the money, he'd invested in his dreams for her. She was just going nuts from missing him so much and angry at him for being dead.

"Useful, Cass, real useful."

To prove her sanity, she forced the rumpled letter back into the envelope, as neatly as possible in the midst of the maelstrom, and she forced that back into her leather pack.

Her father, the self-educated man, also the most well-read man she'd ever met. But she'd learned early on to do her math and science homework before he came home from the fields. His frustration at being unable to help her with them had always been a strain.

Cassidy's mother was a single solitary memory. She'd been standing in the open doorway of the house, leaving on a stormy night to answer a call to the hospital. The wind at the door blew her hair across her face as she leaned on her father's arm. Cassidy's only memory of Adrianne Knowles, a woman with no face. Then Bea Clark rushing in from next door to sit with her.

She and Daddy did talk about the books though. He had sharpened her mind as they puzzled out the books together. Ayn Rand piled next to Shakespeare, Heinlein and Hugo, Dickens and a biography of Jimi Hendrix. Their house was always awash in books. And the massive collection of wine books, thumbed again and again by both of them, the only books to have a proper bookcase, had sat in the place of honor in the living room. Everything else jumbled into stacked wooden crates, mounded on tops of dressers, and enough on the dining table to make it a battle to find room for two plates.

The chill spray of a particularly large wave spattered her with a few drops and the next with a few more.

The tide must be coming in.

She scrambled from her hiding place and rose back into the wind which threatened to topple her down into the roaring waves. She forged her way back up the hill. The wind tore at her backpack and thumped it against her spine. The camera. Right.

She squatted to get out of the wind and pulled out her trusty point-and-shoot. The wind nearly blinded her when she turned back into it. Her hair swirled about her head.

A sailboat.

Two lunatics in a sailboat were off the point of land. A cobalt-blue hull climbed out of one wave, pointing its bow to the sky, and then plunged down and buried its nose in the front of the next wave before rising again in a great arc of spray and green water. Huge, maroon sails snapped in the wind, loud enough to sound like a gunshot above the roaring surf.

Whoever the captain was, he and his buddy were crazy. They must both be male because no woman in her right mind would ever go out into a storm like this. But if they wanted to sail right into her picture, she wasn't going to complain; it was a beautiful boat. At the perfect moment she snapped the photo then turned for the woods and the long trail home.

Other fine romances by this author

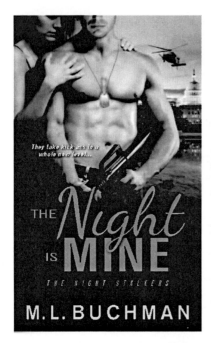

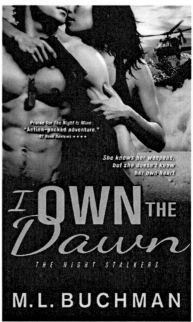

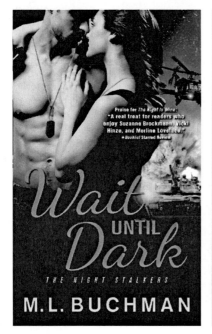

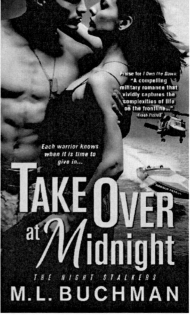

M. L. BUCHMAN

NPR Top 5 Romance Author

Praise for *Wait Until Dark*
"Suzanne Brockmann fans will love this."
- *Booklist* starred review

Daniel's Christmas

a Night Stalkers Holiday Romance novel

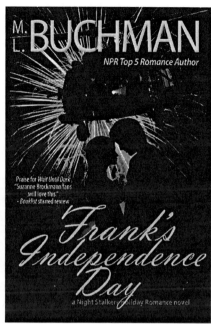

M. L. BUCHMAN

NPR Top 5 Romance Author

Praise for *Wait Until Dark*
"Suzanne Brockmann fans
will love this."
- *Booklist* starred review

Frank's Independence Day

a Night Stalkers Holiday Romance novel

M. L. BUCHMAN

NPR Top 5 Romance Author

PUBLIC MARKET

FARMERS

" Buchman (offers) well-honed
emotional rendering of characters.
Booklist, Take Over at Midnight

Where Dreams RESIDE

an Angelo's Hearth Romance novel

M. L. BUCHMAN

NPR Top 5 Romance Author

ML Buchman writes
with eloquence
and a feel for emotion.
-*Long and Short Reviews,
I Own the Dawn*

Maria's Christmas Table

an Angelo's Hearth Romance novel

Other Books by this Author

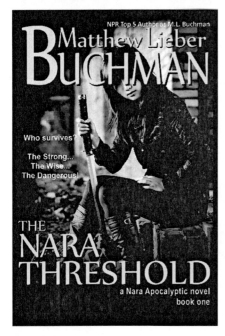

CPSIA information can be obtained at www.ICGtesting.com
Printed in the USA
LVOW07s1830020914

402060LV00002B/594/P